THE CODE

by Peter Lerangis

AN
APPLE
PAPERBACK

SCHOLASTIC INC.
New York Toronto London Auckland Sydney
Mexico City New Delhi Hong Kong Buenos Aires

ISBN 0-439-70242-9

Design by Joyce White

12 11 10 9 8 7 6 5 4 3 2   4 5 6 7 8 9/0
                                                              40
Printed in the U.S.A.
First printing, July 2004

For Tina, Nick, and Joe

Prologue

Eleven. Eleven. Eleven.

On the eleventh day of the eleventh month, they would turn eleven years old.

Evie noticed this first. Of course. She was older, born 3:43 A.M. to Andrew's 3:47 A.M. That meant (by her reckoning) she was also smarter, more mature, and more organized. Eleven was a lucky number, she said, and anything repeated three times was lucky — so this birthday would be blessed twice.

Andrew, not to be outdone, pointed out the Twin Factor — it doubled your luck, so the day would be blessed *four* times.

Whatever. They both agreed it would be a Day of Unbelievable Importance.

The morning broke clear and crisp. Evie, still half asleep, brought her blanket to her chin against the gust through her open window. She adored Saturdays like this. She was dreaming about plans for the day — shopping with Mom, followed by a party at the Ridgecrest Retro Bowlerama — when she opened her sleepy eyes. Facing her, propped up on a batting tee by her bed, was a bloody skull.

"Charming," she muttered.

She picked it up between her thumb and forefinger. It felt cheap. It looked cheap. It still smelled of boy-sweat from Halloween. How *anyone* could wear this mask was beyond her. In fact, most of the time *Andrew* was beyond her.

Evie quietly got out of bed and flung the door open. This startled her brother, who was crouched with his ear to the door. "Waiting to hear me scream?" she asked.

"I was, uh, looking for a contact lens," Andrew said.

"You don't wear contact lenses."

"Mom's contact lens." He turned and ran for the stairs. "*Found it, Mom!*"

"Andrew Wall, what part of 'You are not allowed in my room ever' don't you understand?" Evie ducked back into her room and grabbed the mask. She would pull it down over his head and force him to eat while he wore it. Andrew would *forever* associate Life cereal with the taste of plastic mouth-hole.

She barreled downstairs and charged into the kitchen. Andrew's back was to her, and she ran into him from behind. Evie was bigger and stronger than Andrew, and by all rights she should have knocked him flat. But he just staggered. Didn't even turn around. Didn't say a thing.

"Andrew?" Evie said.

A torn envelope, addressed to both of them, lay on the table. Andrew held a letter in his hand.

"It's from Mom," he said softly.

From upstairs came their father's muffled voice: *"Evie? Andrew?"*

Andrew handed the letter to his sister.

For the next year, she remembered the moment like an image captured on a hidden camera. The sound of Pop's footsteps rushing down the stairs. The washed-out color of Andrew's skin. The way his fingers shook ever so slightly. The sight of the familiar handwriting, usually neat, now hurried and abbreviated on a ripped sheet of yellow legal paper.

Dear ones,

   Oh how I wish I could celebrate "11 11 11" w/ you. When I return we will have another birthday party no matter the day. Pls understand I would not go if I did not have to. I wish I cd say "Be back soon" but I'm afraid this will be a long one. Take care of each other, & know that I love you more than the world.

Love always,
Mom

P.S. You will hear from me soon. And when you do, remember:

11 11 11 :
A picture forms
Without you —
And it's all a jumble.

Chapter One

Enemy sighted, starboard bow.

Bombardier A. Wall sets his infrared goggles. Throttle — open.

We're going in.

Shiiiiiiii! He ignores the wind's shriek, the pull of G forces on his battle-hardened body. Only a slight shift of his chiseled jaw gives an indication of the grim conflict to come . . .

Andrew hopped the curb at the intersection of Elm and Main. Tensing his legs, he rose from the seat of his new mountain bike. It was his pride and joy — a well-oiled and highly sprung machine, camouflage green, custom-built by military-engineer friends of Pop's — and it touched down in the bike lane as if landing on a cloud.

Enemy at twelve o'clock — dead ahead. Hit encampment and bank left!

Andrew leaned left. He strafed the shoe store, blasted the Army-Navy Surplus, dive-bombed the Laundromat, then looped around the front of a lone SUV that was idling at the light.

Mission accomplished. That'll show 'em who's boss!

It was all new — the town (Shoreport), the weather (cold), and the people (New Englanders). Andrew hated moving to new places. It made him itchy and uncomfortable. Sure, he'd racked up plenty of states in his lifetime: New York, Louisiana, California, Alabama, Wisconsin, Idaho, Oregon, and now Connecticut — if it had a military base, he'd lived there. The towns themselves were fine. It was the getting-to-know that was hard. Really hard. Until he mastered the town's little secrets and smells, its shops and odd buildings, until he knew the neighbors and the kids in school, he didn't feel right.

The new bike helped. Evie had one, too, but Andrew's was better. Faster. It made the routine easier, and the routine was essential. It was the same each time, more or less: move into another smallish house, memorize the streets, learn the names of the local stores, try not to insult the general's kid in class.

And most of all, establish control.

Enemy sighted, port side!

"Yo, where'd you get the bike?" a voice shouted.

Twelve, maybe thirteen years old. Tough guy. Short

black hair, big head, surrounded by adjutants. Definitely trouble.

Andrew could hear the hoots and hollers as he banked right and got the heck out of sight. Although he'd never been in Shoreport before, some things never changed.

When you're new, they're always gunning for you.

Andrew shot up the blacktop driveway, slammed on the brakes, and skidded to a stop just before he reached the back door.

"She's still working, Pop!" he said to a pile of cardboard boxes. "Brakes, tires, gears — all perfect."

"She's built to last. Indestructible!" Richard Henry Wall peered out from behind the stack. He wore a white baseball cap to keep the sun from his scalp, which had long ago lost its battle with baldness. In his right hand was a list. Always a list. Andrew's dad loved them — laundry lists, shopping lists, lists of lists. He kept a record of every grade Evie and Andrew ever got. He had a strict daily rotation of clothing, to make sure he wore everything evenly. Moving to a new house? That meant *tons* of lists. Which explained why, on that day, he was very happy. "The movers didn't do too badly this time," he said, reading from a legal pad. "Four broken plates, a couple of lost beach toys, a cracked picture frame. Where have you been?"

"Around."

"You didn't talk to any strangers, did you?"

"Nope. Didn't wet my diapers, either."

Mr. Wall smiled. "Okay, okay. Hey, seriously, it pays to be careful until we're more familiar with the place. Understand? No talking to any strange adults."

"Roger." Andrew saluted.

"Speaking of strange adults . . ." Mr. Wall leafed through his legal pad and showed Andrew a page. Under a neatly typed heading — CHANGE-OF-ADDRESS NOTICES — was a huge list of names in tiny print. Andrew recognized some of his father's colleagues; parents of friends from the last town; scores of people he'd never heard of; and of course, their mom's brother, Frank, who held the honor of being their only living relative. "Can you think of anyone I missed? Friends? Family?"

"Give me a week to look at it and I'll get back to you."

"Thanks!" Mr. Wall rolled up the list and whacked Andrew gently on his bike helmet. "Now, go help your sister unpack, then we'll have dinner."

Dinner? That was two hours away, minimum. Fighter pilots needed to refuel. There had to be food somewhere, snacks left over from the long car ride to Shoreport.

Andrew laid down his bike, ran into the house through the kitchen door, and flung open the refrigerator. It was warm, unlit, and empty — except for a note in Evie's handwriting.

$$🐑 + (L \times W) - A + 2 + L8.$$

"Sheep . . . ?" Andrew muttered to himself.

No. Not sheep. No sentence began with the word *sheep*. It was *ewe*, the code for "you" in Evie's mind.

Next was "L x W." *Length times width . . .*

Math. Ugh. The thought of it gave him the shivers. What did "L x W" measure anyway — perimeter? Volume? Area?

Better to move on. *Minus A.* Well, you couldn't take away an *A* from *perimeter* or *volume*, so it had to be *area*. So. Subtracting an *A* from *area* gave you . . .

Rea?

Andrew thought a moment. Duh. Other *A*. "Are!" he exclaimed, then read the whole thing through. "You . . . are . . . too . . . late."

Ooooh.

She was clairvoyant. How did she know he'd be starving?

His sister was a cruel and greedy mind reader.

"*Evie!*"

He slammed the refrigerator door, raced upstairs, and barged into the front bedroom. Of course, Evie had claimed *that* room, the biggest and brightest, which overlooked a stately maple tree in the middle of the lawn. She had already unpacked, set up her desk, made her bed, assembled her aquarium, and even arranged her stupid dolls. The room had a big modern desk with a drawer that locked. *Andrew's* bags, unopened, were on the dusty floor of a dark room on the side of the house — a room with a tiny closet, a card table, a battered two-drawer file cabinet, and a view of the neighbor's purple-trimmed house. (Who on earth trimmed their house in *purple*? Yuck.)

"Evie?"

She wasn't in her room. He searched his own room and his dad's. No luck. The bathroom was in the rear. It was a small, dark room with a stall shower. The door was open a crack and Andrew spotted a candy wrapper on the floor. He pushed the door open all the way and saw a pile of bagged cookies, crackers, and chips.

Ha. Thought she could hide food from Bombardier A. Wall.

He stepped inside and snatched an open bag of Cheez Doodles.

"SURPRISE!"

A stream of water caught Andrew on the side of the face. Evie was leaning out of the shower, fully clothed, aiming a removable shower head directly at him.

"*Ambush*!" Andrew flung the bag at her, then dove for the floor.

The water stopped. Evie was coated with wet Cheez Doodles, the orange dye streaming down her T-shirt. "Ew . . ."

Andrew howled. "Got you last!"

He moved fast, but Evie was on him in no time. They fell into their dad's bedroom, tumbling to the floor. Andrew felt soggy snacks being shoved down his shirt. He pushed against Evie but she had him pinned. She was *bigger* — that was the worst part. Girls grew faster, twins or not. The world was just unfair.

He kicked at her but missed. With a solid thump, his foot hit the dresser. A framed photo teetered at the edge and fell. Andrew and Evie both lunged for it.

It bounced off Andrew's outstretched fingertips and hit the floor with a crash.

"Now look what you did," Evie whispered.

Footsteps clomped up the stairs from below, and the door opened.

"What on earth . . . ?" said Mr. Wall as he stepped inside. He looked from Evie to Andrew to the mess on the floor. He said nothing, but his eyes did all the talking: *Clean up. Pay for a new frame. Or else.*

As he turned and left, Andrew sighed. "Now we're in trouble."

Evie was already picking up the larger glass pieces. Andrew knelt beside her and carefully picked up the photograph, which was facedown in a pile of crushed wet snack food. He shook off the glass shards and turned it over.

It was a snapshot from their vacation out West two years ago — Andrew, Evie, and their mom standing at the Continental Divide, the geographic center of the country. Andrew was pointing to the left, Evie to the right. Their mom, like the Scarecrow from *The Wizard of Oz*, was pointing both ways, across her body. Her hat was cocked to one side, her head to the other — and she was on the verge of cracking up. In the bright sunlight of the Colorado Rockies, her brown hair was nearly auburn.

"You know what her eyes looked like when she laughed?" Andrew said. "Little crescent moons, upside down."

"You mean *rotated*," Evie said. "Crescent moons are already sideways, so they look the same upside down.

And it's not what her eyes *looked* like. It's what they *look* like. She's still alive."

"How do you know?"

Evie glared at him. "Andrew, I cannot believe you even said that."

Silently she left the room.

Andrew didn't answer. It wasn't that he was disloyal. He was realistic. It wasn't a crime to face the truth — or what *might* be the truth.

Mom was an International Businessperson. That was all they knew. Nothing else, not even the name of her company — that's what they called it: The Company. She had ties to the military somehow, that seemed obvious. Pop worked for the military, in covert operations — and wherever Pop had to move, she always found work. What did she do? Who did she work with? Unknown. She never liked to talk about it. Whenever it came up, the subject always changed.

When he was little, Andrew thought his mother was a professional storyteller, or a movie critic. That's what she liked to do around the house, tell stories and rent old videos. She'd lull him and Evie to sleep at night with amazing tales — King Arthur, Pecos Bill, Cuchulain, Davey Crockett — she knew them all. In another life, she always said, she would be a folklore professor like her wacky brother Frank in Alaska.

That wouldn't have been such a bad life, Andrew thought.

Instead, she was always taking off on some stupid emergency secret assignment. This one was the worst — ten months (and counting) without so much as a phone call, an e-mail, or a letter. Pop had tried to find her. So had Uncle Frank. There were late-night phone calls, visits from detectives. No clues, no signs, nothing. With their luck, she was in some country where the mail was delivered by camel.

Or dead.

Or, worst of all, none of the above.

Maybe, just maybe, she wasn't on assignment at all.

When Andrew thought back to the days and weeks before 11 11 11, all he remembered were shouts and arguments. Sharp words, slammed doors in Mom and Pop's bedroom. Evie had reacted by becoming the good little child. Not Andrew. Every day was something disastrous: fights at school, breaking things around the house, talking back, long bike rides when he was supposed to be working around the house.

Mom and Pop yelled at him. Evie yelled at him. But

that just made things worse. He couldn't help himself. He still didn't know why.

Andrew looked at the photo again. Pop had taken the shot. He had been relaxed and fun-loving then — not the moody guy he'd become since Mom had vanished.

Sometimes, when Andrew thought and dreamed of Mom, he pictured her happy again — but in another house, with another family. Why not? She hadn't been happy in this house, with *this* family.

He hated the image, but there it was.

Andrew blew away tiny glimmers of glass that dusted the photo, then set it on the dresser. He reached into his pocket, took out his blue nylon wallet, and pulled out a battered old business card. CASSANDRA KANE WALL, it said on the front, next to the symbol of The Company: a strange red, white, and blue trapezoid with a yellow slash over the Latin words LIBERTAS, FIDELITAS, PROBITAS — Freedom, Loyalty, Honesty.

He turned it over to read the back — MOMMY ♥s YOU! It was left over from his first-grade lunch box, where she had taped it inside the hinged top. He had found it in the attic when they'd been packing.

"Why are you just *sitting* there?" Evie demanded, bustling back into the room with a broom and dustpan.

Andrew looked up from the card. "Why did she do it, Evie?"

"Why did who do what?"

"Mom. Why did she leave us?"

"Job assignment. You know that." Evie began sweeping up the glass. "She left because she had to, not because she wanted to."

That's what he expected her to say. That's what she always said. But just the fact that it was on her mind meant *something*.

Chapter Two

"White, white, white, white, white, light brown, white, light blue, white, light brown, white, white, white ..." Evie called out, as she and her brother turned from Locust Drive onto Sycamore Street. It was Labor Day, and Evie *had* to investigate every street in the neighborhood before school started.

"Thank you for the color lesson," Andrew said, pedaling alongside her. "But I was there that day in kindergarten."

"This town is the worst," Evie replied. "Boring house, boring house, boring house. Same three colors, same two designs, same lawns, same landscaping."

Andrew had to admit she had a point. Shoreport was like a collection of Monopoly houses, some facing front, some sideways. Each lawn had one tree exactly in the center — as if some weary Johnny Mapleseed, passing through town on a tree-planting mission, had run out of imagination.

Still, Andrew thought, *you don't have to give in.* If

you made the right mental adjustment, you could be any-where. A steaming Costa Rican jungle, a Russian village during World War II, an Indonesian rice paddy — it was a matter of attitude.

Plus, it was cool to be stared at like you were a celeb-rity, which always happened when you were new in town.

"Cool bikes," a girl called out from the front steps of a nearby house. She was blonde and solid-looking. Some kind of athlete, Andrew figured. She was listening to a portable CD player and reading magazines with two friends.

"Thanks," Evie said, circling slowly in front of the house. "I'm Evie, and this is my brother, Andrew."

"Charlotte," the girl replied. "But everybody calls me —"

"Toilet," said one of the other girls with a giggle.

"Ignore her, she's demented," Charlotte said, slap-ping her friend playfully. "It's Char."

Evie laughed. "Nice to meet you. See you around!"

"Pop says we're not supposed to talk to strangers," Andrew reminded his sister as they pedaled toward their house.

Evie rolled her eyes. "He means *adult* strangers. Your

problem is, you don't *want* to talk to new people. It's good to be social, Andrew. We can't just ignore everybody. They'll think we're snobs. Besides, a little human contact makes this neighborhood less dreary."

"There's a girl named Toilet on our block. And this makes things *better*?"

They were approaching their house now. As they swung onto Lakeview Avenue, Andrew caught a flash of color that he hadn't noticed before.

The house next door — the one with the purple trim — didn't have much of a lawn, but its gardens brimmed with life. On the left side, reds, oranges, greens, and purples cascaded from the porch into a vibrant pool of multicolored plants. On the right, closer to Andrew and Evie's house, was a vegetable patch where tomatoes hung like small moons over dozens of thick squashes. A narrow herb garden was tucked among the vegetable plants, giving the air a spicy aroma.

"Nice." Andrew laid his bike down. He stood at the edge of the garden and leaned over the herbs, taking a deep breath.

Behind him, Evie said, "Andrew . . ."

He heard the slam of the front screen door.

A white-haired woman headed down the front porch

steps toward him. She was tying the cord of a floppy wide-brimmed hat beneath her chin. She was dressed in jeans, a purple tie-dyed T-shirt, and purple running shoes.

"Those plants are *very* fragile!" she snapped.

"Sorry!" Andrew squeaked.

"And bikes on my property give me the jitters," she continued. "You never know where they're going to land."

"Yes, sir," Andrew replied. "I mean, *ma'am*!"

He picked up his bike in a hurry and pushed off.

"At ease," he heard the woman say as he and Evie hightailed it into their own driveway.

"She's creepy," Evie said, reaching into the refrigerator for a snack.

"Nah, she's just old and cranky — but she'll get used to us." Andrew headed for the front door.

"Where are you going?" Evie asked.

"To get the package on the porch," Andrew replied.

"It's a holiday. There's no mail delivery."

"Oh, really?" Andrew opened the front door and pulled in a parcel about the size of a shoe box. It was wrapped in plain brown paper with a computer label that read EVELYN AND ANDREW WALL. "Must be special delivery," he called out. "Didn't you see this? I did, back when we were running for our lives. My eyes are *always* open. Even during a crisis."

Evie came in, her mouth full of peanut butter and crackers. "Sonsh."

"In English, please."

Evie swallowed. "Strange."

The postmark was a handwritten squiggle across a row of stamps. In the upper left corner, someone had drawn a huge, hollow F with a return address written inside. An address from Alaska.

"Uncle Frank?" Evie guessed.

"Guess so." Andrew grinned. This had to be the work of Uncle Frank the Folklorist, Mom's brother. He liked to collect odd gifts whenever he traveled, and then send them to Evie and Andrew when they moved to a new house. Last time it was a wax candle in the shape of a double-decker bus from London. And before that a cheese sculpture of the Eiffel Tower that smelled like old socks. He had been in Africa, on safari, according to the last postcard they'd received, so maybe this was a rhino horn — or was that illegal? Andrew began ripping the box open eagerly.

"No!" Evie cried out. "We should wait for Pop. What if it's *not* from Uncle Frank?"

"It's addressed to us, not Pop," said Andrew. "And it's from Alaska, where Uncle Frank lives."

"Still, we don't *know*. What if it's dangerous?"

They both stared at the box. "Tick . . . tick . . . tick . . ." Andrew whispered.

"Boom," Evie said.

And Andrew tore off the wrapping.

Chapter Three

It wasn't cheese. It wasn't a double-decker bus. Or a rhino horn.

Andrew and Evie went upstairs and spread out the objects on Andrew's bedroom carpet — a green kaleidoscope with a white ring, a package of seeds, and a manila envelope containing a shiny gold key. "Looks like Uncle Frank is cleaning house."

"Why would he send these things to *us*?" asked Evie. "I had a kaleidoscope like this when I was *six*. He knows we're older than that. Seeds? A key? What's so African about this stuff?"

Andrew picked up the kaleidoscope and looked through. It was heavier than he expected, and instead of a color display it showed a circle of dim whitish light that shifted as he moved the tube. He pointed it at the living-room window and turned the white ring. Slowly the house across the street came into view. "Hey, it's a telescope!"

Evie yawned. "Have fun examining the roof shingles.

I'll be in my room IM-ing my friends about our exciting life."

As she did that, Andrew experimented. He pushed the focusing ring away from him. The house across the street seemed to race closer. A zoom lens! Impressive.

He zeroed in on their mailbox.

THE MICHAELSES'.

Andrew smiled. This telescope was perfect for detective work.

If Evie wasn't interested in this stuff, fine. He'd keep it in his room. He began repacking the box, carefully tucking in the telescope, the seeds, the key, and the shreds of paper and plastic used as packing material.

He almost didn't see the envelope.

It was stuck against the inside of the box — sealed shut, with no markings on it at all.

Andrew held it to the light. Inside was a letter, typed. Slipping his finger under the flap, he opened it.

```
            A Silent Cry
      Alas!  My  dear,  distant,  dis-
   tracted little ones don't hear as I
   speak. Am I not loud enough? No, I
   realize to my chagrin that they're
   too far. In another world. I sigh,
```

and then all of a sudden, I spy
something that I cannot adequately
describe. "I'll tell, to you only,
of this violet bird's splendors," I
say to the two children. "It has
intelligence and will sing for
you — so go to where it is, I beseech you! I am afraid, though,
you'll need all your energy and
charm to make it understand who you
are." I look to see if they understand me; I'm not certain.

I can't help but notice foxglove
afoot. "This gift will be available
to assist if you know how to find
it," I say. "The plant and bird,
you see, are identical. Whatever
grows the closest to one's home may
be useful. Be careful, though. Like
William Tell, who certainly had no
intent, one presumes, to cause harm,
the people nearest to you may prove
ultimately to be your undoing."

With these words I leave, frus-
trated but not without hope — even

with my doubts. Father Christmas I don't expect for another few months, but the weather has turned cold and I must leave for a while. Like that fabled jolly old saint, I will parcel things out. Don't rush and don't worry — these words may, we'll agree, be the wisest that can be said — along with Marlon Brando's advice from ON THE WATER-FRONT: Keep fighting. Always be a contender. Gain strength together.

It's too soon to know if I affected the children. Love, as you know — more than stories about birds and plants, myths and movies — works miracles. A picture forms, but confused, because you are missing.

I spy, you spy. X marks the spot.

Weird.

Andrew tucked the note into the box. "Evie," he called out. "You have to see this! Something else from the box."

It took Evie a few minutes to come to his room. "This

better be worth it," she said as he handed her the letter. "I had to make an away message." She read it quickly, her eyes narrowing. "You interrupted my conversation for this? It's dumb. And wrong. Marlon Brando was much better in *A Streetcar Named Desire,* anyway. And he didn't say anything about being a contender. Rod Steiger did. Mom must have rented that a hundred times."

"It *was* Brando," Andrew insisted. "Mom used to imitate him!"

"Can I go back to my friends now?" Evie asked.

"I think it's kind of cool. Like a fable, or a story. Does Uncle Frank write short stories?"

Evie handed Andrew back the sheet and headed out of the room. "He should stick to cheese sculptures."

As his sister left, Andrew flopped back on his bed. He read the story again, carefully. There was something mystical and odd about it. But also something familiar.

He couldn't figure out why.

Chapter Four

"Hi, Evie!" called Char as she unlocked her bike from the school rack. "Want to ride home together?"

Evie sat on her bike near the playground gate, balancing on one foot. It was the end of the first day of school, and the skies threatened rain. Her dad had given strict instructions: Always come home together, don't leave your brother alone, don't talk to any strangers, go right to your homework. "Not today, sorry," Evie said. "I'm supposed to wait for Andrew. He's really shy around new people. He'll freak out if I leave."

"No prob," Char replied as she got on her bike and began to pedal away. "See ya!"

"*Andrew!*" Evie called for what must have been the hundredth time.

She spotted her brother halfway across the playground, zigzagging through the crowds on his bike. His earnest scowl meant one of two things: He was pretending to be Luke Skywalker attacking the Empire stronghold, or World War II Bombardier A. Wall saving the world from destruction. Whatever it was, he was nearly plowing into kids left and right.

Switched at birth. That *had* to be what happened with him. He belonged to another family. From Mars, maybe. Even as a baby, he was *nothing* like her. Her earliest memory was the sight of Andrew in the crib, talking to his toes. From there he progressed to conversations with his bottle, his pillow, and his stuffed animals. Hardly ever with other kids.

Even now, Andrew couldn't talk to new people in a normal way. He had to be something else, someone else. Someday, if they were lucky — maybe at age thirty — Andrew might discover reality.

Count your blessings, she reminded herself. The new school had put them in different homerooms. Their only classes together were English and Math.

And that was fine with Evie.

"Nyeeeeeeaaaaarrrrrr . . ." Andrew screamed, pedaling toward her.

Bombardier. Evie recognized the sound effect. Now he was swerving around a tough group of boys. She recognized a couple of them from her homeroom. The ringleader was a big kid who always seemed to be eating chocolate. His name was Dino Bouloukos, but everyone called him Baluko.

As Andrew passed, Baluko stuck out his leg.

Andrew yanked his handlebar in the other direction. He swerved, leaving a black skid mark on the playground. With a sickening *shhhhh*, the bike slid out from under him and he fell.

Evie dropped her own bike and ran toward him. "Are you all right?"

"It's just a flesh wound," Andrew said as he staggered to his feet. The left leg of his pants was ripped from the knee down.

"I'll give you more than a flesh wound next time, Speed Racer," Baluko said. "You almost ran into me. My dad is a lawyer. If you ever touch me with that bike, I'll sue the pants off you."

"Take the pants now," Andrew suggested. "I can't wear them anymore."

"Funny guy," Baluko said, placing one foot on Andrew's fallen bike. "What's a dork like you doing with a bike like this?"

"Get your big fat foot off that," Evie said.

A couple of Baluko's henchmen guffawed. "Ooh, is that your girlfriend?" said one.

"She's my sister," Andrew replied. "And don't get her angry, she's a black belt in sumo wrestling. Get ready, Evie, we're going to have to jump these guys."

Evie nudged him in the ribs. "Shut up," she whispered.

"Did you say *jump*?" Baluko began hopping up and down on the spokes of Andrew's rear wheel. "No problem."

"Stop!" Evie rushed toward him, pushing him away.

Andrew picked up the new bike. Its chassis was scratched and its rear wheel was hopelessly warped. "This is brand-new, custom-made!"

"Guess I just broke it in," Baluko said, already walking away with his pals. "Oh, and you can keep your pants."

"They wouldn't fit over your fat butt, anyway!" Evie shouted.

Andrew waited until Baluko was out of earshot before he muttered, "I'll get that big jerk next time."

Evie picked up her bike and scowled at him. "None of this would have happened if you hadn't nearly run him over!"

"I couldn't help it," Andrew protested, as he tried to walk his wobbly bike toward the gate. "He was in the way of the bombing of Dresden."

On the way home, Andrew and Evie left the damaged bike at the shop for repairs. The cost would equal four weeks of Andrew's saved-up allowance. Not to mention a huge scolding when their dad found out what had happened. But Evie pointed out that the neighborhood had a lot of lawns, and they'd all need mowing. He could make up the money in a week — two, tops.

One problem. To work in the neighborhood, you had to get to know the neighbors. Convince them to hire you. Both of which were about as much fun for Andrew as walking on nails. He was already off to a miserable start with the neighbor with the garden. And Baluko.

Of course, it was easier to meet people if you knew a little about them in advance.

For that, Andrew had a plan. He barged into Evie's room with the green tube from Uncle Frank's box. "I think we should survey the territory. Do a little neighborhood research."

"With a kaleidoscope?" Evie asked.

"It's a telescope," Andrew replied. "A powerful one."

Evie scowled at him. "And this strange desire excuses you from having to knock at my door?"

Andrew knelt by her open window and trained the telescope across the street. Outside, the sun had begun to set. A few younger kids were playing catch with a baseball, and lights were flickering on in several houses. "Looking into a person's house is a perfect way to pick up information."

"You mean, *spying* on people?" Evie said. "That's sneaky. That's rude. That's unethical!"

"Mm-hm . . ." he said, adjusting the telescope's focus on the living room of the house across the street. "Ah-ha. *Fantastic!*"

"What? What's going on?" Evie grabbed the telescope and looked through it herself. "I see a mom watching TV and feeding a bowl of mush to her kid. If this is your idea of fantastic, I am deeply worried about you."

"It's not what you can *see*, Evie. It's what you can learn. One: Both parents in this family work — the dad's in the military and the mom has a civilian job. Two: They are well educated. Three: The mom is a basketball player and the dad plays piano semi-professionally. Four: The woman you see is not the mom. She's a hired babysitter. Five: She's Greek."

"How do you know all that?"

"They have a two-car garage, which is empty. That tells me that the parents are out and they've hired a baby-sitter. They spell their name correctly on the mailbox — Michaelses', with an *es* at the end, followed by an apostrophe. No one gets that kind of thing right, and that shows a good education. The pictures on the wall show him in a uniform and her in regular clothes. I counted at least four basketball trophies on the fireplace mantel — and the statuettes are female. And there's a piano against the wall, with lots of sheet music stacked on top and a large pair of men's slippers tucked near the pedals."

"And the woman, who you think is a baby-sitter?" Evie asked.

"She's fiddling with a string of beads in her left hand — worry beads. The Greeks use them all the time. Alexandra Anagnostou brought them to school last year as a souvenir, remember?" Andrew raised an eyebrow. "Or were you absent that day?"

Beep-beep!

A car puttered slowly into Evie's range of sight. She zoomed back to get a fuller view of the street. It was a bright purple Volkswagen bug. The driver waved to the ballplayers, who scattered to let her go by. "Hi, Mrs. Digitalis!" one of them called out, as the VW swerved into the driveway next door.

"Garden-lady alert," Evie said.

"She has a purple *car*, too?" Andrew said.

"And a weird last name." Evie put down the telescope and bolted up from the window. "Let's get a closer look."

They both ran into Andrew's room, which had a clear view of their neighbor's house. She had parked in the driveway and was now climbing out of the car. She wore a loose-fitting dress with a purple-and-white pattern and atop her head was a baseball cap labeled SHOREPORT GARDEN CLUB. As she walked around to the trunk, a fastball from the street came zinging toward her head.

"Heads up!" one of the kids shouted.

Mrs. Digitalis spun around. Her left arm darted upward, and she plucked the errant ball out of the air without flinching.

"She's quick," Evie muttered

Andrew took the telescope from Evie. He focused it on Mrs. Digitalis as she pulled from the trunk a large carton of paper that read COPY PAPER — 10 REAMS. It looked heavy, but she hoisted it to her shoulder as she walked toward her front door.

"Strong, too," Andrew said. "I'm guessing she's an ex-hippie turned Olympic weight lifter."

Evie rolled her eyes. "I have to finish my homework and make dinner. It's my turn and we're having chili — and no cracks about calling the poison control center. Call me if you spot her in the house."

"I don't think so," Andrew replied. "You wouldn't want to be sneaky, rude, or unethical."

As Evie huffed back to her room, Andrew cleared off his desk. On the first day of school, the homework mainly consisted of writing your name in your new notebooks. For Andrew, however, this was a design opportunity.

He was halfway through making his math notebook cover into a Martian village when a dim rectangle of reflected light appeared on his wall.

Andrew turned. The light was coming from a room on the second floor of Mrs. Digitalis's house. Inside, behind sheer, gauzy curtains, she was walking about purposefully. Her hat was off and her white hair hung loose past her shoulders.

Andrew quickly cut off his light and ran into Evie's room. "Target spotted," he said.

They both scurried back and stood at the window. In a corner of Mrs. Digitalis's room, a blue computer screen came to life. Andrew focused the telescope on it, but the angle was tricky. "What do you see?" Evie asked.

Andrew zoomed in. After the computer booted up, Mrs. Digitalis made a window appear on the screen. It was a folder chock full of icons. One by one, Mrs. Digitalis highlighted the icons and made them disappear. "She's deleting files," Andrew said. "Tons of them."

"Can you read the file names?" Evie asked.

"Too far away."

One by one, Mrs. Digitalis carefully emptied several Windows folders — every single icon. Then she clicked on what appeared to be the Recycle Bin and emptied that, too. When she was finished, she turned to a tall metal file cabinet and yanked open a drawer. She hauled out a stack of hanging file folders and put them on her desk.

Quickly she removed small stacks of paper from the folders and lowered them out of sight, below the window-sill. Through the open window, Andrew heard the faint whir of a motor: *dzzzit . . . dzzzit . . . dzzzit . . .*

"I think she's using a shredder," he whispered.

Mrs. Digitalis held a report in her hand now. As she removed the clear plastic cover, Andrew focused on the top sheet. On it was emblazoned a red, white, and blue symbol with a yellow slash running through it. "And it looks like she works for the government," Andrew added. "The logo is everywhere."

Evie grabbed the telescope from his hands and peered through. "Andrew, that's the symbol for The Company!"

"How do you know?" Andrew asked.

"It's obvious! Look at the shape!"

"A *lot* of government group symbols look like that," Andrew replied. "Can you see the words — tacos, Tostitos, quesadillas . . . ?"

"Quesadillas?"

"The *Latin* words! You know, the ones on The Company's symbol?"

"Libertas, fidelitas, probitas," Evie snapped. "And I can't tell whether or not I see them."

"Let *me* try!" As Andrew lunged for the telescope, the front door thumped open and shut downstairs.

"I'm ho-ome!" their dad's voice rang out.

Andrew dropped the telescope. He and Evie fumbled for it on the floor, but Andrew snatched it at the last moment.

He looked outside just in time to see the white edge of the report in Mrs. Digitalis's hands disappear beneath the windowsill.

Chapter Five

The Department of Defense.

The FBI.

The CIA.

The Army, Navy, Air Force, Marine Corps.

Andrew clicked from Web site to Web site. None of the symbols was exactly like the one on Mrs. Digitalis's computer.

It had been nearly twenty-four hours since he and Evie had spied on Mrs. Digitalis, and he couldn't get that stupid symbol out of his mind. Andrew always imagined that younger people worked for The Company — smart, alert, athletic types like Mom. Not gardening old ladies.

Still, you never knew.

He called up a search engine, typed "libertas fidelitas probitas," and waited.

Nothing.

He heard the door open behind him. "So . . . have you decided?" Evie asked.

"Decided *what*?" Andrew replied.

"What you're going to say about your bike, Sherlock," Evie said. "Pop's started making dinner. You're going to have to tell him something."

"I wasn't even thinking about it." Andrew looked over his shoulder at his sister. "What's the problem? I didn't tell him yesterday. He didn't notice it was missing."

"So you think if you stay quiet, he just won't figure it out?"

"Every day, he's gone before we leave and home long after us — maybe he *won't* figure it out."

"Kids?" came their father's voice from the kitchen. "Can you come down and set the table?"

Andrew bolted out onto the landing above the stairs. A warm, lemony smell wafted up from the kitchen. As he bounded downward, he took a deep whiff. "Mmm, smells good. It'll be great to have your cooking for a change, Pop."

"What about my chili last night?" Evie asked, coming in behind him. "You ate a bowl. Pop had two."

"He must have taken the antidote beforehand," Andrew said.

"Not funny!"

"Heartburn never is."

Mr. Wall pulled a steaming plate of pork chops from the oven. He was wearing a blue apron over his work clothes. "Please stop fighting. I could hear you arguing upstairs. Do you ever stop?"

"I didn't start it," Evie said.

"You did so!" Andrew protested.

"All I did was come into your room and ask about the bike!"

Dumb. Stupid. Loudmouth. Andrew grabbed a basket of rolls and ran to the dining room.

"Bike?" said his dad. "What happened to the bike?"

"It's busted," Evie announced. "It's going to cost forty dollars to repair and get a new tire."

"*Evie, you weren't supposed to —*" Andrew glanced at his dad, then quickly away. "Some kid stepped on it yesterday."

Mr. Wall's tired expression had grown cloudy. "What was it doing on the ground?"

"He was dive-bombing the kids," Evie said. "They retaliated. They knocked it down. But it was Andrew's fault."

"It was *their* fault," Andrew protested. "They're bullies. Terrorists of the playground. I should have invited them for the dinner you made last night. *That* would have shown them."

Mr. Wall rubbed his fingers on his forehead. "I have had a long day. Can we *please* eat in peace?"

"Fine," said Evie, storming into the kitchen.

Andrew sheepishly followed. He helped serve the pork chops. He sat down to eat with a smile. He tried to start conversations.

Across the table, Pop and Evie were the two new Dwarfs, Silent and Grouchy.

Andrew was in mid-chew, on the last bite of his pork chop, when he heard a car door thump outside. Glancing over his shoulder, he saw the purple VW bug pull away from the curb, fast.

"Mrs. Digitalis must be late for the Garden Club meeting," Andrew remarked.

Mr. Wall lowered his fork. "Mrs. Digitalis? You've gotten to know this woman?"

Evie gave Andrew a dirty look. "*Now* who has the big mouth?"

"Okay, I *know* we're not supposed to talk to strangers, Pop, but she's our *neighbor*," Andrew protested. "Besides, we didn't *get to know* her. We didn't even say hi. We were looking at her garden, and she yelled at us."

"We know her name because we heard someone else call her Mrs. Digitalis," Evie went on.

"We will continue this discussion later," Mr. Wall said wearily, rising from the table. "I have to go back to work for a couple of hours."

"We'll save you some dessert," Andrew said.

Clearing his plate, Mr. Wall left the dining room. He was out the back door in seconds.

Evie shot upstairs and into her room.

Andrew had dessert all to himself, but he didn't eat a thing.

Libertas . . .

Fidelitas . . .

Andrew doodled idly on a scratch pad.

What he should have been doing was his English homework. But reading "The Pit and the Pendulum" was not exactly a laugh riot on a night when you were alone in your room after dark. As it was, he felt on edge. Evie had already cackled at one too many IMs in her room, and Andrew's knees were bruised from jumping with fright in his desk chair.

When a square of light appeared on his desk, he nearly screamed.

It was a reflection from a window in Mrs. Digitalis's house. The light in her living room was on. Then the light in her computer room turned on, too.

Weird. He hadn't heard her return home.

He glanced out toward the front of the house. The VW was not there.

"Evie, come here — quick!" Andrew called out, grab-

bing the telescope. As he knelt by the window, Evie's footsteps thumped into his room. "The lights are on, but she's not home."

"Duh, she has a *timer*," Evie replied.

A shift of light. Movement.

Andrew trained his lens on the living room.

Yes. A shadow. Moving quickly left to right. "Someone's in there," he said.

Evie knelt next to him. Outside crickets began to chirp. A dull hum sounded from the power lines.

There. By the couch.

A man. Balding, dressed in gray. Kneeling.

"See him?" Andrew whispered.

Evie nodded.

Through the screen window the man looked blurry, like a TV image. He pulled the couch away from the wall and crawled behind it.

"What's he doing?" Evie asked.

"I don't know," Andrew replied.

"Andrew, look. Upstairs!"

Andrew lifted the telescope. The computer in Mrs. Digitalis's study was on. Sitting in front of it was a young-ish woman — dark hair, pulled back into a ponytail. As a splash screen glowed on the monitor, she turned toward the window.

Andrew and Evie ducked.

Slowly Andrew counted to twenty, then peeked again. A curtain had been drawn across the study window. It obscured the details of the room. Still, he could see the outline of the woman sitting at the computer. Her fingers flew across the keyboard.

"Robbers," Evie said.

"No kidding." Andrew put down the telescope. He could see both rooms now, both intruders. "But one of them is behind the couch and the other is at the computer. What are they stealing?"

A pickup truck rumbled past. Then an SUV, going the other way.

And at the same time, a car pulled up to the curb and stopped.

The VW.

"Uh-oh . . ." Evie whispered.

Mrs. Digitalis hopped out of the car, gently closed the door, and walked toward her house.

"She can't go in there," Andrew said. He raced out of the room and into Evie's. Her aquarium stood on her dresser, neatly set up but dry. He grabbed a handful of colored pebbles and brought them back to his room.

"She's on the porch," Evie said.

Andrew couldn't see Mrs. Digitalis. She was obscured

by the roof of her front porch. At this angle, if he aimed just right, he could get the pebbles into the porch through the side.

At least it would get her attention.

Andrew opened his window fully. He leaned out and threw. The pebbles landed with a soft clatter — some rolling down the porch roof, some making it through the opening and onto the porch floor.

For a moment nothing happened. Inside the house, the burglars continued, intent on whatever they were doing. They hadn't heard.

Then Mrs. Digitalis appeared, leaning out of the porch, looking upward.

Evie caught her glance and frantically pointed in the direction of Mrs. Digitalis's living room.

The old woman's face tightened. She nodded and backed away, out of sight.

"I'm calling nine-one-one," Evie said, darting out of the room.

Andrew watched the front lawn. Any minute Mrs. Digitalis would be running across. Back to the VW. Of course, she'd be smart enough not to interrupt the crooks. She'd hightail it to the police.

But the car stood by the curb, unoccupied.

He heard a soft click from under the porch roof—a door opening.

Andrew ran to the top of the stairs. "Hurry, Evie! She's going inside!"

"*I can't find the cordless phone!*" Evie called from downstairs.

As she clattered around, looking for the phone, Andrew ran back to the window. Mrs. Digitalis was in the living room now, tiptoeing across the carpet. She knelt on the couch, her white hair spread across her shoulders.

The man rose, startled. He tried to come out from behind the couch.

Mrs. Digitalis shoved the couch toward the wall, pinning his legs. With a quick move, she held him against the wall with her right arm.

The dark-haired woman from upstairs ran into the room. She appeared to be shouting something.

Mrs. Digitalis lifted the man's shirttail over his head — until the shirt, half on and half off, trapped his arms and prevented him from seeing. Then she shoved him toward the door.

In a moment, both burglars were stumbling across the front lawn. As the woman struggled to pull down the man's shirt, she glanced up.

Andrew ducked again. But not before making eye contact.

"I can't find the phone!" Evie said, racing into the bedroom.

"It's okay," Andrew replied. "Our neighbor can take care of herself."

He rose to look out the window. The robbers were gone, and Mrs. Digitalis had shut the front door and vanished into her house.

But the young woman's eyes, dark and intense, seemed to hover above the lawn. Still looking at Andrew.

Chapter Six

"A-choo!" said Evie, mounting her bike to go to school early Monday morning.

She looked next door. Mrs. Digitalis was bent over her vegetable patch, not reacting to the sound at all.

"That was the fakest-sounding sneeze I ever heard," Andrew said.

"She hasn't said a word to us all weekend," Evie hissed. "Hasn't *looked* at us. Those burglars were after something — computer files, whatever. Obviously she's a really high-level person. Maybe she even works for The Company. We foiled the robbery *and* saved her life. She owes us!"

Andrew tested his brakes and shoved forward, swinging his legs over the frame. It felt great to be riding again. Pop had been pretty reasonable about the bike. On Saturday afternoon he'd slipped Andrew a loan — "payable weekly out of future earnings" — and Andrew had picked up the bike from the shop, good as new.

"We didn't save her life," Andrew said, pedaling down

49

the street. "Mrs. Digitalis would have whupped them without my help. Those burglars were in more danger than she was."

"Still," Evie grumbled, "not even a little thank-you note? I mean, *you* put yourself in danger. The burglars saw your face. You're a witness. What if they come back to rub you out? Your death will be Mrs. Digitalis's responsibility."

"Thanks a lot, Evie."

Usually Andrew had no problem ignoring Evie's statements. Today he found himself glancing at the faces of every dark-haired woman they passed.

At the school bike rack, a boy with bright red hair pulled up next to Andrew.

"Cool bike," he said.

Andrew gave him a look. He seemed okay — tall, skinny, friendly smile. "Thanks. It's custom-made."

"Yeah? Mine's a Schwinn. Sixty bucks at Wal-Mart. Hey, I'm Jason."

"Uh-huh." Andrew nodded.

Evie rolled her eyes. "His name is Andrew. Andrew Wall. If he's forced to be himself, he doesn't know what to say to new people. I'm his sister and translator, Evie. Bye."

As she disappeared into the crowd heading for school, Jason said, "She's funny."

"Hysterical," Andrew replied.

"Where'd you get the bike?"

"My dad knows some engineers who like to build stuff like this. So they did."

"Does that mean there's none other like it in the world?"

"I guess not."

Jason ran his finger along the frame. "Wow. You could get a fortune for it."

A couple of other kids had gathered around and were staring at the bike, too. Andrew very carefully pulled a tissue out of his pocket and began dusting the bike off. "I'm never selling it. I love riding it too much — it's kind of like cruising on air. The frame's made of a special alloy used on space shuttles. It's really light."

"*No fooling*?" a familiar voice called out. Baluko was barging through the crowd. He stuffed a Chunky into his mouth, pushed Andrew out of the way, and lifted the bike off the ground. "Hey, it *is* light. Maybe we should see if it flies!"

Jason stepped forward and grabbed the bike by the frame. "Drop it, Baluko."

"Who's going to make me?" Baluko asked.

"Someone already did," Jason shot back, "and probably regrets it."

A few kids in the crowd snickered. "So funny I forgot to laugh," Baluko said.

"So clueless you don't know how," Jason replied.

The onlookers fell silent. Red-faced, Baluko tried to shove the bike to the ground. But Jason had a firm hand on it.

"You're lucky, Wall," Baluko grumbled, turning away. "Really lucky. There's always someone else to fight your battles . . ."

As Baluko sauntered into school, the other kids began scattering to class.

"Thanks, Jason," Andrew said. "You have guts."

"Me?" Jason laughed. "He could have whupped me *so* bad. I was shaking."

"You sure didn't show it," Andrew said.

"It's a trick my dad taught me." Jason started toward the school door. "Never show 'em you're afraid. Even if you are. Simple. They back down. Works every time."

Andrew fell into step beside his new friend. "Well, you can be the first person in history, besides me, to try my bike — after school today, if you want."

Jason's face lit up. "All riiiight!"

As they went inside and headed for their separate

homerooms, Andrew felt a tug of envy. *It's a trick my dad taught me*, Jason had said.

Andrew tried to think of tricks his dad had taught him.

His mom had been the one who coaxed him into riding a bike and braving a roller coaster. She'd held him up in the water until he wasn't afraid to swim. She'd read stories with him, waited patiently while he sounded out words, helped him choose clothes that other kids wouldn't laugh at, talked to him about his shyness and how to make friends, convinced him a hundred times that people didn't really hate him.

Pop? Well, he was good at helping with math homework. And he sure worked hard at his job. Evenings and weekends, too. So maybe he didn't have too much tricks-teaching time. It wasn't his fault.

Still, there had to be something he had learned from his dad.

Andrew was still thinking as he entered homeroom.

After school, Jason was waiting in the front lobby. "I'm ready for that ride!" he said.

"Ride?" Evie said, walking up behind them. "Andrew? You don't need me to hold your hand on the way home?"

"No, but you can take my books," Andrew said.

"Ha-ha," Evie said, walking off. "See you on Comedy Central."

Andrew and Jason headed around the corner to the bike rack. "I ride my bike all the time," Jason said. "It's like flying — like you said before. Sometimes I pretend I *am* flying. Like on a broomstick or a magic carpet."

"Really?" Andrew replied. The more he talked to Jason, the more he liked him. "I pretend I'm somewhere else, too —"

He swallowed his words as his eyes focused on the spot where he had left his bike.

It was gone.

Chapter Seven

"Pop is going to kill you," Evie said. "No. He is going to have a fit, force you to do one hundred push-ups every day, dock your allowance, make you clean the house top to bottom, cut off TV privileges from now till college — and *then* kill you."

"Thanks for the pep talk," Andrew replied. He plopped down on the front porch step.

"It wasn't his fault," said Jason, who had walked home with Andrew. "He locked up the bike."

"No, I didn't," Andrew mumbled, pulling the bike lock from his backpack. "I forgot. I got distracted."

"Okay, it *is* your fault," Jason said.

Andrew shook his head. "It's the *thief's* fault, okay? I'm the victim."

Evie paced the porch. "And the thief is Baluko. Has to be. We need to do something. We'll storm his house. We'll call the cops to back us up."

"I thought *I* was the one who lived in a fantasy world," Andrew said.

"Hey, we don't know for sure that Baluko did it," Jason reminded them. "We don't have any evidence."

"So we'll catch him riding the bike," Evie said, "take a photograph, and *then* press charges."

"I have to go home and take care of my little brother," Jason said, "but I live near Baluko. I'll keep an eye on him. If I see the bike, I'll let you know."

"Sure," Andrew replied, dropping his head into his hands with a heavy sigh.

As Jason rode off, Mrs. Digitalis emerged from her house and began tending her herb garden. Evie watched her through the chrysanthemum bush with silent attention. "We have to meet her," she suggested.

"How can you think about her now?" Andrew muttered. "My bike was just stolen."

"We can't do anything about that now," said Evie. "But we can work on getting Mrs. Digitalis to talk to us."

"How can we? She hates us," Andrew said.

"Don't be paranoid. Maybe she just hates everyone."

"That's encouraging." Andrew lifted his head and watched Mrs. Digitalis for a moment, then ducked behind the porch wall, pulling Evie with him. "She saw us. I think."

"Why are we hiding?" Evie asked. "We could just say hi."

"If we want to meet her — really meet her and make friends — we should make a plan," Andrew suggested, happy to be distracted from the misery of his missing bike. "Break the ice. Bring her a peace offering. Something she would like."

"I'm all out of purple shirts," Evie said.

"Something for her garden, I mean. Like a pink flamingo."

Evie thought for a moment. "A tool, maybe — a trowel or a weed whacker. Wait. Don't we have some seeds?"

"Pop bought a watermelon, I think. She could grow a watermelon tree."

"No. The seeds from the package Uncle Frank sent us. Remember? You didn't throw them out, did you?"

"Nope." Andrew raced into the house. Evie followed him upstairs and into his bedroom. He took the box out of his closet and reached in for the seed packet. He examined the photo on the front — three purple-red, bell-like flowers sharing a common stem. "They're nice," he remarked.

Evie read the label beneath the image. " 'Foxglove.' I like the name."

"Foxglove . . ." Andrew said. "I've heard that name before."

Evie shrugged. "Probably from some dumb war video game."

"What if she already has these flowers?"

"It's the thought that counts," Evie said. "Come on."

They went downstairs and out onto the porch. Evie led the way down the front steps and over to the house next door.

Mrs. Digitalis was still working in her garden. She barely looked up as the twins arrived. "Yes?"

"Hi," Evie said. "We were just wondering . . . if you're okay."

"I hope those robbers didn't mess up your house," Andrew continued.

Mrs. Digitalis finally stood and faced them. "I suppose you never can be too safe, even in a neighborhood like this," she said. "Thank you for warning me. I do appreciate your vigilance."

Evie held out the seed packet. "Here, we brought you something."

Mrs. Digitalis's expression softened. "Foxglove?" she said, taking the gift. "How . . . interesting."

"If you already have some, we can get you something else," Andrew squeaked.

"No, no, I'm . . . surprised, that's all. It's a thoughtful

gift, a lovely flower, suitable for every garden. I shall plant them immediately. Foxgloves are the type of seeds you plant in late summer . . ." As Mrs. Digitalis tore open the packet and peeked inside, her voice trailed off. Something flickered across her face.

There's a dead cockroach in there, Andrew guessed. Now she would really hate them.

Mrs. Digitalis glanced up, her eyes looking deeply into Andrew's face and then Evie's, as if noticing them for the first time. Quickly she closed up the packet. "What am I saying? You gave me a gift and I am being so dreadfully inhospitable. Surely you'll come inside for a snack? I'm Alicia Digitalis, by the way. And you're . . . ?"

"Evie and Andrew Wall," Evie replied.

"Wall . . ." Mrs. Digitalis said.

"Maybe you know our cousins — Stone, Brick, Berlin, and Wailing," Andrew said. "That's a joke."

"Actually," Evie said, "we'd love to join you, but we're not supposed to talk to strangers. Our dad said so."

Mrs. Digitalis smiled. "But my dears, we *are* on a first-name basis. I hardly think we're strangers any longer. Besides, I'm *sure* he would see no harm in your visiting an elderly next-door neighbor. I promise to take full responsibility."

Evie looked at Andrew. "Well, okay," she said.

They followed their neighbor inside, passing through the living room. It was spare and modern — white walls, white furniture, white bookshelves, and a white patterned rug on a blond-wood floor. The sofa was back in its regular place as if nothing had happened.

Mrs. Digitalis led them through a dining room with a low glass table, little more than ankle-high, surrounded by cushiony mats. The kitchen, like the rest of the house, didn't have much decoration — a few utensils, some standard-looking pots and pans, that was it. No fancy copper bowls, wineglasses, artwork — not even a HOME SWEET HOME needlepoint.

Mrs. Digitalis brought out a bag of baked veggie chips, a box of carob-chip cookies, and a bowl full of long, shriveled-up brownish strips. "Dried seaweed?" she asked. "It tastes better than you think."

Out of politeness, Evie gave the seaweed a try. When she began to turn slightly green, Andrew decided to opt for the cookies. They weren't much better.

Mrs. Digitalis walked to a corner of the kitchen and flicked on a little machine. It made a noise that sounded like static. "White noise," she said. "I find it soothing. Very karmic."

Andrew nodded, his mouth full of veggie chips. "Sounds like a car vac."

"Okay, time to be honest," said Mrs. Digitalis as she sat at the kitchen table. "Let me take a good look at you. This is quite a surprise, meeting you here. I didn't recognize you at all, until you told me your names. You're a lot older than the most recent photos I've seen."

"Ph-photos?" Evie said.

Mrs. Digitalis nodded. "You were wearing a striped shirt, Andrew. And you, Evie — a yellow pastel-patterned bathing suit. You were little children. And now you're almost teenagers."

Andrew nearly choked on his cookie. He knew the picture. "That was from three summers ago, on Stimson Beach. We were both nine years old."

"Mom carries that photo in her purse," Evie said. "It's her favorite."

"Yes, she does," Mrs. Digitalis said. "She showed it to me at least three times."

Evie fell silent.

Andrew swallowed. The cookie went down his throat like a wad of steel wool. He looked at his sister, who now seemed as white as the rest of Mrs. Digitalis's house.

"You *know* our mom?" he said.

"Oh, yes. In fact, I've met you two before, in New York City — one Christmastime, I believe — you were quite small." Mrs. Digitalis sighed. "You must miss your mother dreadfully."

"We do," Evie said.

Andrew had to tell himself to breathe. Could this woman — this total stranger — actually *know* Mom? What were the odds of that?

"How well do you know her?" Andrew asked. "Do you know where she is?"

Mrs. Digitalis leaned forward. "You must keep your voices down. I believe I do know something about your mother's whereabouts — but I'm not certain yet, and even if I were, I wouldn't be at liberty to say. It is no co-incidence that you are here, in this town, in this house."

Andrew shivered. Suddenly the kitchen felt very small. And cold. "*Who are you?*"

"A friend," she replied. "For the moment, that is all you need to know. I will help you as much as I can, if you will agree to four things. One: You must help me, too, whenever you feel you can. Two: You must never ask me where your mother is, because I can't tell you. This is es-sential. Three: You must not mention a word of anything we say to anyone — and that includes your teachers and your friends. And especially, I'm sorry to say, your father.

If you break these rules, you put yourself — and your mother — in great danger. Is that understood?"

Andrew and Evie nodded in agreement.

"And number four?" Evie asked.

Mrs. Digitalis looked slowly from one to the other. "No matter what happens, no matter what anyone tells you, you must trust me."

Chapter Eight

"Evie, I am not going to sit through home videos," Andrew said, pacing across the den. "I say we call Pop right now. There are laws against people like Mrs. Digitalis."

Evie's eyes were on the TV screen. She was fast-forwarding through an old tape. "She knows Mom, Andrew."

"She *says* she does," Andrew replied. "How do we know she's telling the truth? Maybe she's been spying on *us*!"

"We have to trust her," Evie said. "I do. And I can *prove* we met her. Look — here it is! Remember this? Uncle Frank took this video . . ."

She pressed the PLAY button on the remote and the sped-up image slowed down — colored lights, a thick, heavily decorated Christmas tree, a small apartment. Carols played in the background, along with the sound of clinking glasses and laughter. Mom had been assigned to a job in New York City for one winter, when Andrew and

Evie were four. It was one of those times when they had to live apart from Pop, who'd stayed on the military base.

Andrew remembered the apartment only vaguely, but he could not forget this party. "I don't want to see this," he said, turning away.

"Come on, you're not a baby anymore," Evie reminded him.

On the screen, little Andrew was scurrying down a long hallway to answer a ringing doorbell. He was clutching a toy train. The door was brand-new, reinforced with steel. The glass eyehole had not been installed yet, leaving a hole through the door. Mom had stuffed it with a black sock. The person ringing the bell, impatient now, decided to poke the sock through. On the video, it resembled a long black snake wriggling through the hole — which is exactly what it looked like to a little boy racing toward the door.

"*Aaaaaaeeeeehhhh!*" Little Andrew's shriek was bloodcurdling.

"This is so embarrassing," the older Andrew moaned.

"Just watch." Evie's eyes were on the door in the video. It opened. In walked the visitor.

Had Uncle Frank captured her face?

"Oh my goodness, what happened?" The voice was

muffled, barely audible behind the screaming. The camera was shaky, too, lurching right to left as Mom and Pop squeezed past Uncle Frank to tend to Andrew and the visitor.

There she was. There *someone* was. Standing in the door. Wearing a beret, large glasses, and a down coat.

"See?" Evie said. "It's Mrs. Digitalis!"

"Rewind and stop the frame," Andrew said.

Evie reversed the action. They both leaned forward as she used the SLO-MO button on the remote. When the visitor was on-screen, she pressed PAUSE.

Andrew squinted at the screen. "How can you tell it's her? I can't. It's blurry. It could be a man. It could be a monkey with a hat."

"I'm *enhancing* the image with my memory," Evie said. "And I can see her face. Don't you remember what she looked like?"

"Are you kidding? I was busy running from the Snake That Ate New York."

Evie pressed the PAUSE button again and the screen came to life with an image of Mom cradling a shaken Andrew in her lap, drying his tears. She looked up crossly into the camera, at Uncle Frank, waving him away. "No one needs to see this," she said.

The screen went blank and Evie turned the video off.

"I'm convinced. Mrs. Digitalis said she met us at Christmas. I think this was the time."

"No way," Andrew replied. "The image was too blurry. You just *want* it to look like her. Evie, think about it: What's the chance we'd end up in a house next to someone who *happens* to know Mom — and *just possibly* where she might be? It's too much of a coincidence."

"This is a military town. Mom works for The Company, The Company's tied to the government, the government's tied to the military. We always run into people who know Mom and Pop in these places."

Andrew shook his head. "It smells funny. All this hush-hush stuff. First of all, if Mrs. Digitalis knows where Mom is, why won't she tell us — or Pop? Second of all, why did she make us disobey Pop about talking to strangers? Grown-ups don't do stuff like that. They're loyal to each other — it's like a club. Third, she flings grown men up against walls with one hand and doesn't report a burglary to the cops . . . and she expects us to *trust* her?" He stood up and peered through the window. "She's in that room, e-mailing her pals again — 'Heh-heh-heh, really scared those good-fer-nuthin' kids tonight, Myrtle!'"

"But if she's making it all up, how would she know Mom was missing?" Evie asked.

"She didn't. All she knew was that we *had* no mom —

she could see that. Think about what she said to us: 'I met you in New York City at Christmastime.' Lots of people go to New York City around Christmas."

"But she described that old photo from Stimson Beach in exact detail. She knew what we were wearing."

"Every parent has beach photos. She just guessed. She couldn't have gone wrong. If she said my shirt was red and your bathing suit was blue, we would have remembered another photo —"

"Manhattan Beach, in Los Angeles!" Evie exclaimed.

"Exactly. She's playing mind games. She wants revenge because we drive her nuts. We ride our bikes up her driveway, get too close to her garden, throw rocks at her . . ."

Evie thought about it for a moment. Sometimes Andrew made sense. Sort of.

But sort of not.

Even if Mrs. Digitalis *was* angry, would she really torment kids who missed their mother? Were people really that cruel?

There was more to it than that. There had to be. "If Mrs. Digitalis really knows about Mom, there's hope," Evie said. "We're closer to Mom than we've been in almost a whole year."

"We don't need hope," Andrew replied. "We need evidence."

"Hope is good, Andrew. It can lift you up."

Andrew nodded. "I don't want to be lifted up. It makes the fall harder."

"Andrew, what if Mrs. Digitalis really knows where Mom is? What if she *can't* tell us where?"

Andrew's face had darkened. He was staring off into space, looking as if he were going to cry.

"Andrew? What's wrong?" Evie asked.

Her brother didn't answer for a long moment. "Sometimes," he finally said, "I imagine Mom *happy* to be away from us. I see her in another state, in another house. A place where people don't argue as much."

"You think she . . . ?" Evie let her voice trail off. She did not want to go where this was leading.

"If there's another guy . . . then no wonder Mrs. Digitalis wants to keep the secret from Pop," Andrew said.

Evie shook her head. Mom did not — *not* — run away with another man.

The thrum of a car engine made them both look out the window. Headlights illuminated the driveway as their father's car glided past the TV room toward the garage in back of the house.

"Evie," Andrew said quietly, "if Mrs. Digitalis is keeping secrets — no matter what they are — Pop needs to know, too. We have to say something."

Grimly, Andrew and Evie greeted their dad at the door. Pop seemed tired and quiet as he walked to the kitchen. "No dinner?" he grumbled.

"Sorry," Evie said. "We didn't have time."

"Thank goodness for the microwave," he replied, taking three frozen dinners out of the freezer. As he prepared them, Andrew and Evie set the table.

Evie waited to speak until they were all eating their meals. "How was your day?"

"Same as always," Pop replied. "And you? Did you ask great questions in school?"

"Speaking of questions," Evie said tentatively, "we ended up asking our neighbor a few of them."

"Oh?" Mr. Wall said.

"Mrs. Digitalis invited us inside today," Andrew added.

"We said no," Evie said, "but she insisted —"

"Technically, since we *had* talked to her before, she's not a stranger anymore, just a harmless old neighbor," Andrew continued, "so we knew you wouldn't mind . . ."

Mr. Wall gave them both a stern look. "I have not had the pleasure of meeting her yet. Until I do, I expect you to do as I asked."

"But why?" Andrew pleaded.

"People on the fringes of the military — retirees,

people who perhaps have been pushed out, who can't let go of the organization — they tend to make trouble," Pop said. "They grasp. They stretch the truth. To make themselves feel important again, the way they were when they were young. Now, look, what's done is done. But no further visits to Mrs. Digitalis. Am I understood?"

"Yes," Evie and Andrew said in unison.

"Do I have your promises?"

"Yes," they repeated.

"Good."

Andrew played with a forkful of mashed potatoes. He had no appetite. "Pop?" he said. "Can I ask you something?"

"Of course," Pop replied, opening the newspaper to the national section.

"What did — *does* — Mom do for a living?"

"International business."

"I mean, what exactly?" Andrew pressed. "What's her job?"

"Negotiations, public-private interfacing, government regulatory oversight —"

"What does that *mean*?" Evie blurted out.

"I would tell you," Pop said, "but then I'd have to shoot you."

Andrew smiled wanly. It was an old military joke. An old, sick military joke. "Pop, is she ever coming home?"

But Pop was intently reading the paper. Once he did that, there was no use pressing him. He had checked out for the evening.

Chapter Nine

Tuesday morning Andrew left for school at 7:15 A.M. — way earlier than usual, because he had to walk. Evie would be leaving later by bike. He waited until his dad left, slipped through the back door, and walked alongside Mrs. Digitalis's house.

Her car was in the driveway. An elaborate, new-looking keypad lock system was mounted beside her garage door. The front and rear doors to her house sported brand-new locks behind thick metal plates. On her front lawn was a small octagonal sign that read KRIME-GARD: THIS HOUSE IS ALARMED.

The locksmiths must have come during school on Monday. Right. Of course. What do you do after a robbery? You call a locksmith. You secure your house. You file a police report.

Police. Had Mrs. Digitalis ever contacted the police? Andrew hadn't seen them. He would have, too, if they had come. He'd been home most of the weekend. Maybe they also arrived yesterday during school, like the lock-smiths.

No. Cops didn't wait until Monday to do business. They were available 24/7 if they were called.

If.

Why *wouldn't* she call the police?

Was she hiding something that even they couldn't see?

Andrew glanced back at the house. A soft clacking came through the open window of Mrs. Digitalis's second-floor computer room. She was working.

Working on what? Andrew wondered. *Destroying more files? What does she have up there? What were those robbers after?*

Andrew was in a daze when he walked into school.

"Bingo," Jason said, coming up behind him on the way to homeroom. "He's got it."

"Who's got what?" Andrew asked.

"Baluko has your bike!" Jason replied. "I rode past his house about fifty times this weekend. Never saw a thing until Sunday afternoon. That's when the minivan pulled away with the whole Baluko family inside — I counted them. Eleven."

"Eleven?"

"They brought their pet chimpanzees and their goat. Just kidding. Seven. Anyway, I sneaked into their yard and looked through the garage window. There's a big canvas tarp covering a woodpile. Looks like it hasn't been touched for centuries — but it has! The front wheel of your bike was poking out."

They paused outside the homeroom door. "This is *great,* Jason," Andrew said. "I'll break in someday when the family's gone."

Jason shook his head. "Can't. That's illegal."

"I'll confront him, then. I'll tell him you saw it through the garage window."

"And get me in trouble?"

"Well, what do *you* think I should do?"

Jason thought a moment. "Get him to *give* it back to you. Offer him something in return. Something he wants and you don't need. Something he can't say no to."

A gallon of chocolate-chip ice cream.

A coupon for free meals at the local fried-chicken place.

A book of secret codes to his favorite computer game.

Andrew thought about it all day, but he couldn't come up with anything. The walk home was hard. Hard on Andrew's head, as he tried to think of bribes for Baluko. Hard on his body, because it was a long haul with a backpack loaded with books.

And potentially hard on his butt, if Pop were to find out the bike was missing.

When he got home, all that was in the fridge was a bottle of prune juice, a plastic tub of old carrots in water, and an open pack of tofu dogs. In the sink lay a soggy, empty container of ice cream.

"Thanks for leaving me some!" he called upstairs to Evie, but she was in her room, yakking on the phone, oblivious to the rest of the solar system.

Andrew went into his own room, shut the door, threw his backpack on the floor, and wondered if malnutrition was a good excuse for not handing in homework.

Under the bed, Uncle Frank's box peeked out, next to Andrew's safe.

A telescope.

That would be a perfect trade for his bike. Baluko would love it.

Quietly Andrew leaned down and lifted the box onto his bed. Glancing out the window, he could see Mrs. Digitalis walking around on the second floor of her house.

If he was going to lose the telescope, he might as well put it to good use while he still could.

He reached into the box. As he pulled out the telescope, the note came out, too. It dislodged the key, which fell to the floor with a solid thunk.

He leaned down to pick it up, closing his fingers around the jagged ridges.

They gave. Just a bit, but he could feel it.

Odd.

Andrew held it to the light. It looked like an ordinary key, maybe a little heavier than usual — but when he squeezed the ridges, hard, they pushed inward. When he let go, they sprung out.

The head of the key was a disk shape with a scored circumference, like the edge of a quarter. On a hunch, Andrew dug his fingernail between two of the scores and pushed down. It was some kind of circular switch. When it moved, the key's ridges moved, changing the key's shape.

An adjustable key. What a concept.

Andrew reached into his closet. From under a pile of shoes, he pulled out another safe. No one in the world knew about it. Not Pop. Not Evie. Inside it were three things — the toy train Mom had given him on that fateful Christmas depicted on the videotape, a photo of Mom and him from fifth-grade graduation day, and the shopping list Mom had put on the fridge the night before she left. He wished he had her letter, but it had disappeared. Next to the safe's handle was a hefty lock hanging from a thick hasp.

He tried to insert the key but it wouldn't fit. Slowly he adjusted the circular switch.

Shhink. In it went.

The lock snapped open.

He tried the key on his bike lock.

Snap.

Open, too.

"Evie?" Andrew called out. "Hey, Evie!"

Andrew barged into her room. She didn't notice, mainly because (a) her back was to him and (b) her conversation with Char about sockwear was too urgent for petty interruptions.

Quietly Andrew inserted his key into Evie's locked desk drawer.

Click.

He pulled. The drawer was stuck.

He yanked it again. With a sudden jerk, the whole thing came out — and fell to the floor in a shower of envelopes and papers.

"*Andrew, what are you doing?*" yelled Evie. She said a quick good-bye to Char and slammed the phone down.

Andrew knelt to pick up the papers. Many had hearts with initials on them and arrows through them. "What the — ?" he muttered.

"*You leave my stuff alone this minute. Your spying has gone too far and give me back my desk key!*" Evie screamed, sweeping the papers up into her arms.

"That's my point! I don't *have* your key, Evie —"

"You're a liar," she said, lifting her mattress. "You didn't take anything else, did you?"

"You keep your desk key under your mattress?" Andrew asked.

"*None of your business!*"

"Evie, the key came from Uncle Frank's box! It opens any lock."

Evie cocked her head. "Really?"

Andrew led her into his room and demonstrated the key on his other locks. "I wasn't spying on you. I just wanted to try this on your desk drawer and I didn't want to disturb your fascinating intellectual chat."

"Once again, please," Evie said, "and this time without sarcasm."

"The key is fantastic. All of the stuff in the box is."

Evie nodded, lifting out the objects, one by one. "Everything looks like one thing but is really something else." She held the telescope up to the light and pointed to a set of holes on the side of the eyepiece. "Andrew? What's this?"

"A place where you can attach a tripod or something," Andrew replied.

Evie fiddled with it. She pressed a tiny rivet just above it.

Snap.

"What was that?" Andrew asked.

Evie slid open a tiny compartment. Inside was a tinier set of circuits and a wafer-thin disk. "It's a camera."

"You think so?"

"These holes are for a USB connector, Andrew. You hook it up to your computer. I bet you can transfer photos directly."

"Let's *take* some photos, then." Andrew took the telescope and turned toward Mrs. Digitalis's house.

On her study window, a sheet of white paper blocked the view.

"Uh-oh . . ." Andrew trained the telescope on it and read:

A   125
B   142857
C   167
D   2
E   25
F   333
G   5

Come, now, you two: you must
   1   2   3   4   5   6
"C" beyond the surface. Believe you
  7   8   9   10   11   12
me, the skill will pay off
13 14 15 16 17 18
sometime soon.
   19   20
— A. D.
P.S. You want to be spies? Figure out
my code. Hint: If you don't overthink,
you'll solve it in a fraction of the time.
It's all in the patterns.

Andrew sank onto his bed. "She knows we're spying!"

"I am sooo embarrassed," Evie groaned.

"What are we going to do?"

Evie took the telescope and read the message. "We're going to copy this down and figure out what the heck she's trying to tell us."

Chapter Ten

After school the next day, Andrew quickly got his coat from his locker, slammed it shut, and ran down the hall. He liked the lockers in Connecticut. Nice and wide, for thick winter clothes. He took a right and another right, into a corner of the school he rarely visited.

Baluko was kicking his locker door closed. It was bent in the middle from abuse and hard to close due to being jam-packed with papers and coats. "You should probably clean out your locker," Andrew remarked.

"I should probably kick your butt," Baluko replied.

Andrew watched as Baluko hooked his lock into the hole and clicked it shut.

It was a key lock. Perfect.

"Too bad you don't have a combination lock," Andrew said. "The one you have is so easy to pick."

Baluko sneered. "Go home, you're breathing my air."

"I could open it in five seconds."

"You and what dynamite squad?"

"If I prove I can, what's it worth to you?" Andrew asked.

Baluko thought for a moment, then grinned. "If you do it, you get a Snickers bar. If you lose, you buy me a *box* of Snickers — no, a box of Snickers and a box of Twix. Both. *And* you write my English paper for me."

"You drive a hard bargain." Andrew pulled the key from Uncle Frank's box out of his pocket and tried to insert it into the keyhole, but it didn't fit.

Baluko burst out laughing. "You better get me an A+ on that paper, Wall!"

Andrew patiently rolled his thumb down the edge of the key head. He waited for the ridges to move just enough.

The lock fell open with a solid click.

Baluko's face fell, too. "How'd you do that?"

"Magic key," Andrew said, dangling it in front of him. "Opens any lock in the world. In the universe. Now, where's that candy?"

Baluko pulled a flattened, half-melted Snickers bar out of his front pocket. He thrust it toward Andrew, then held it back at the last moment. "First you have to tell me where you got it."

"That information has a price, too," Andrew said.

"Okay. This Snickers bar — *and* a Milky Way." Baluko

reached into his rear pants pocket. "Uh, it's in here some-where . . ."

Andrew's stomach turned. "No deal. I need some-thing more than that."

Baluko eyed him warily. "Like what?"

"You keep the candy and give me — oh, I don't know . . . my bike?"

Evie had been home from school for an hour, and she was still staring at Mrs. Digitalis's note.

It was a code. That much was clear. Letters and num-bers at the top. In a pattern. That was one of the clues. A pattern was involved. But what?

125, 142857, 167, 2, 25, 333, 5. She was good at number patterns — but this made no sense at all, small numbers going to huge numbers and back again ran-domly.

Soon her eyes began to wander. They settled, as al-ways at times of confusion, on her mattress. She wanted so badly to reach under it and pull out her treasure.

But that was a distraction, too.

If you don't overthink, you'll solve it in a fraction of the time.

"A fraction of the time . . ." Evie murmured.

Then, slowly, the answer dawned on her.

She began to write. And write.

When she heard the back door open, Evie grabbed the papers on her desk and flew downstairs. "I have great news, Andrew!" she shouted, barreling through the kitchen.

With a broad grin, Andrew opened the door for her. "My good news first," he said, gesturing toward his bike, which rested on its kickstand by the garage.

"Whoa," Evie said, "how did you manage to get it back?"

"Simple." Andrew grinned. "I gave him that key. You know, the one Uncle Frank sent us?"

"*What?*" Evie snapped. "Oh, Andrew. Just when I thought it was safe to respect my brother's mental capabilities —"

"We don't *need* it —" Andrew reasoned.

"Great, Andrew. Just great. Now Baluko's going to pick every lock he can get his hands on. Shoreport's first wave of robberies ever. You'll be arrested for aiding and abetting the creation of a criminal."

"It was the only thing I could think of! What were *we* going to do with it?"

"That key is valuable," Evie said. "Uncle Frank must have sent it to us for a reason. And if he didn't, if he sent it by mistake, it's still *his*, and we have to return it!"

"Hey, if he wants it, he'll call us. And *then* I'll figure

out a way to get it back." Andrew grabbed the handlebars of his bike and wheeled it into the garage. "Meanwhile, I am locking this with a combination lock. Now, what was your good news?"

On the picnic table, Evie spread out her copy of Mrs. Digitalis's message. Next to it she placed a sheet with her own notes. It had two columns, and when Andrew returned from the garage she covered the right one with her hand so it looked like this:

A   125
B   142857
C   167
D   2
E   25
F   333
G   5

"This was on top of Mrs. Digitalis's note," Evie said. "It's some kind of key — a code. She gave two clues: Number one — 'It's all in the patterns.' Do you see a pattern here?"

Andrew stared at it for a long time. "Well, A comes before B, which comes before C . . ."

"With the *numbers*, Andrew! Never mind. The second

clue is 'you'll solve it in a fraction of the time.' *Fraction.* Well, I said to myself, every fraction is also a decimal. So I fooled around with decimal points, and — *tada!*"

She pulled away her hand and revealed the rest of the paper.

A   125   .125 = 1/8
B   142857   .142857 = 1/7
C   167   .167 = 1/6
D   2   .2 = 1/5
E   25   .25 = 1/4
F   333   .333 = 1/3
G   5   .5 = 1/2

"I still don't get it," Andrew said.

"Look at her message, Andrew. What's funny about it?"

A   125
B   142857
C   167
D   2
E   25
F   333
G   5

Come, now, you two: you must
1   2   3   4   5   6
"C" beyond the surface. Believe you
7   8   9   10   11   12
me, the skill will pay off
13   14   15   16   17   18
sometime soon.
19   20

"The numbers under the words?" Andrew said.

"And the use of the letter C to mean 'see'! She did that on purpose. It's an instruction. It refers to the letters at the top of the page. She's saying, 'apply code C.' Which is . . . ?"

"One hundred sixty-seven . . . also one-sixth!" Andrew said.

"Now look at the way she wrote the message. How many words on a line?"

Evie watched Andrew's face.

"Six words on a line . . ." he murmured.

"And if you read every sixth word — the beginning word of each line . . ."

Andrew read carefully. "Come . . . see . . . me . . . sometime . . ."

"Yyyyyes!" Evie replied.

"That's her secret message to us? 'Come see me some-time'? Why didn't she just write it? What's with the com-plicated code?"

Evie shrugged. "Maybe, when we see her, that's what she'll tell us."

"Shouldn't we answer her?" Andrew asked.

Evie ripped out a sheet of legal paper. "Let's get started."

A half-hour and three shouting matches later, they had a coded response.

"G," what a time to do what
you may suggest later.

"Okay, I think we're ready," Evie said. " 'G' means 'Use the G code,' or the number 5 —"

"Translated into decimals it's point five — in frac-tions, one-half," Andrew added. "So she should know to read every second word."

"What . . . time . . . do . . . you . . . suggest?" Evie muttered. "It's a work of genius."

Andrew glanced skeptically at the message. " 'What a time to do what you may suggest later'? That's a lame sentence."

"We're kids," Evie argued. "What do you expect?"

They waited until they could see Mrs. Digitalis in her room. Then Evie put up the sign.

Mrs. Digitalis looked at it and disappeared. In a moment, she pasted a reply in her window:

*Sounds to me like a
backward ETA.*

"What the heck?" Andrew said.

Evie took out her legal pad and began scribbling. "Let's see. She used the word 'a.' That would be code A . . ."

But Andrew shook his head. "Impossible. That would mean every eighth word. There aren't eight words in the message."

"So what do you suggest, Inspector Gadget?"

Andrew stared and stared. He was tired. His mind was Baluko-depleted. "Maybe it's easier. Maybe it's, like, obvious. You know, when she says 'backward,' for instance. Maybe you spell something backward . . ."

"Like, 'backward ETA'? Hm. Well, ETA stands for Estimated Time of Arrival. That would be . . . Lavirra . . . fo . . . emit . . ."

Andrew bolted upright in his chair. "ATE, Evie. ETA

backward is ATE. The message, decoded, is 'Sounds to me like ATE'! What word sounds like 'ate'?"

"Eight!" Evie blurted out. "Eight o'clock!"

Evie held up eight fingers and they looked out the window.

Mrs. Digitalis smiled and gave them a thumbs-up.

Chapter Eleven

"We're fine, Pop," Evie said into the phone. "Doing our homework . . . the frozen beef stew was yummy . . ."

Andrew put his fingers in his mouth as if he were going to puke. One thing about Pop working late — dinners were even worse than when he was home.

Andrew glanced at the digital clock over the stove. 7:55.

"You'll be home at nine?" Evie smiled at Andrew. "We'll be getting ready for bed. Bye!"

Evie hung up. She jumped away from the phone and grabbed a legal pad and a pencil. "We have an hour."

"We're getting ready for bed at *nine*?" Andrew asked.

"I just said that to make him feel good. Let's go!"

She turned toward the back door, but Andrew grabbed her arm. "Wait. Let's think about this. I mean, she asked us to come over — and boom, we said yes. No questions asked. We still don't know what she wants from us or who she is!"

"She wants to help us, Andrew," Evie snapped.

"But we lied to Pop," Andrew said. "We promised him —"

"That we'd be getting ready for bed, which is true. By nine o'clock we *will* be. Besides, if we help bring Mom back, Pop will forgive every bad thing we ever did." She darted over to the hall closet and threw on a fleece jacket. "Are you coming?"

Andrew sighed. There was only one thing worse than getting in trouble for disobeying Pop.

Getting in trouble for letting Evie go to Mrs. Digitalis's house alone.

He put on his coat and slipped out the back door.

As they crossed Mrs. Digitalis's back lawn, they could see her puttering in her kitchen. Through the screen door they could smell cinnamon and cloves.

She answered before they knocked. "Come in. Come in."

"We have until nine," Andrew said.

Andrew and Evie sat at the kitchen table. Spiced apple cider was simmering on the burner and a loaf of bread was in the oven. Mrs. Digitalis wore jeans and a loose-fitting tie-dyed shirt. Her hair was pulled up in a bun, and a pair of half-glasses rested on her nose.

She set the kitchen timer and flicked on her white-noise

machine. *Karmic,* she had called it. *Abnormal* was the word that came to Andrew's mind. What kind of person needed to listen to *that* all the time?

"Would you both like cider?" Mrs. Digitalis asked.

"Yes, please," Evie replied.

Evie looked comfortable, sitting there with her legal pad. Andrew tried to make himself feel comfortable, too. But this whole thing didn't feel right. Normal people didn't write codes in windows for kids or lure them over against their dad's wishes. Normal people didn't swear kids to secrecy or drop strange hints about their missing mom.

Normally Andrew *hated* "normal." But Mrs. Digitalis made him nervous. What did she want? She had to want *something* from them. As she puttered at the stove, all he could think about was Hansel and Gretel and the witch in the gingerbread house.

He had no intention of drinking or eating *anything* she served.

With a grandmotherly smile, she brought a tray with three steaming mugs and a loaf of bread to the table. "Pumpkin bread," she said. "A famous family recipe, brought over from Norway."

"Digitalis is a Norwegian name?" Evie asked politely.

Mrs. Digitalis lurched a bit as she set the tray down.

"Ouch! Oh, goodness, I spilled cider on my thumb. My, that's hot."

She went to the sink and put her thumb under cold water.

Andrew gave Evie a glance.

"You children are very, very bright," Mrs. Digitalis continued, looking over her shoulder. "I gave you some tough codes. I didn't think you'd get them."

"So why'd you give them to us?" Andrew asked.

"Because you fancy yourselves to be spies. I see you using your telescope. Military-grade photoscope-80-500X Model 0394T. Doesn't look like much, but it's a sophisticated instrument. Where did you get it?"

"It came in the mail," Evie replied. "From our uncle."

"That's some uncle," Mrs. Digitalis said. "Did he send any other interesting goodies?"

"The foxglove seeds . . ." Evie fidgeted, but Mrs. Digitalis's gaze didn't waver. "And also a little —"

"Note," Andrew cut in. He did not want Evie to mention the key. Mrs. Digitalis didn't need to know about that. She was asking a lot of questions. Prying. "That's all, a funny kind of note that didn't really make much sense."

"Perhaps it's in code," Mrs. Digitalis suggested.

Andrew nodded cautiously. "I thought about that."

"Uncle Frank is a little weird," Evie said.

"Mm-hm," Mrs. Digitalis said. "Tell me, have you taken photos with the telescope? You know, you can compress it to fit neatly into your fist. Takes a little practice aiming the lens, but at that compression it goes thirty-five-millimeter wide-angle, so you get most everything — high-res digital photos compressed onto a chip the size of your fingernail, which you can download through a USB cord into your computer."

"Maybe Uncle Frank is a spy," Evie mused.

"Believe me, one fancy spyglass does not a spy make," Mrs. Digitalis said. "If you're serious about spying, you're going to need other techniques."

"Is that what you do for a living?" Andrew asked. "You're a spy?"

Mrs. Digitalis sat at the table and sipped her cup of cider. "No, I'm not a spy," she said, "merely a retired civil servant. But I worked in intelligence. Domestic and international codes were my specialty."

"Does our mom do that kind of work, too?" Evie asked.

"Hundreds of people employed by the government have been sent to study with me — from the lowliest clerks to the highest intellects in charge of our national security. Your mother is among the latter. She has a keen mind —

very gifted with codes. She used them all the time. Clearly she has passed her gifts to you. Already you've discovered Step One in code breaking. Most codes work with a key, or more than one. It can be a number clue, as mine was. It can also be a sentence clue, or a riddle."

"Like, 'a backward ETA,'" Andrew said. "I got that one."

"Very good. In a cryptic sentence, certain words are really instructions. 'Backward' means you need to spell a word backward. 'Mixed-up' or 'scrambled' may mean you have to rearrange the letters of a word. 'A mixed-up glare,' for example, might mean 'large.' Do you understand?"

"Scrambled loco!" Evie said. "That means 'cool!' Get it, Andrew?"

Andrew gave Evie a look. "Reverse hud. That means 'duh.'"

"You both have a knack for this," Mrs. Digitalis interrupted. "Although you could use a few intelligence-gathering lessons. Such as how to observe people so they don't know you're watching. You lack skills in that area."

Andrew sank into the chair. "You saw us?"

"Rule Number One," Mrs. Digitalis continued. "If your room is very dark and that of the people you are spying on is not, they will not see you. If yours is lighter, they will."

"Oops . . ." Evie said.

"The lens at the corner of the window was a good tip-off, too. You should have turned off the lights and closed the door. You see, people do not expect to be spied upon. If you give them no reason to suspect, they will not notice. You can follow someone in a car — right behind him — and on average, he will not notice for approximately *seventy-three miles* of driving. But if you keep two car lengths behind, you can follow him across the entire country . . ."

As Mrs. Digitalis went on giving advice and talking about her adventures, Evie asked questions and took pages of notes.

Andrew couldn't concentrate. Mrs. Digitalis knew her stuff, but still. . . . For someone so smart — someone who specialized in *intelligence* — she did some pretty careless things. Like letting Evie and Andrew see her destroying her files. And if those files were so important, why would she leave her house vulnerable to robbers in the first place?

"Andrew?" Mrs. Digitalis finally said. "You're not listening to me. Is there something wrong?"

Andrew's tongue felt like sandpaper. "Mrs. Digitalis, on the day before the robbers came, we . . . happened to see you in your room. It looked like you were destroying files. Did you know — ?"

"That you were watching? Yes, I did, but it didn't concern me. I was in a hurry. I'd had an inkling that someone was after my files. Alas, it's a hazard of my business."

"Then why did you wait until after they broke in to get new locks for your house?" Andrew asked. "And why didn't you call the cops? Didn't you care?"

Evie stiffened. "Andrew, you are so rude," she said out of the side of her mouth.

"No, it's a good question." Mrs. Digitalis tapped her cup, staring into the liquid for a few moments. "Sometimes, Andrew, if people want something of yours badly enough, it's wisest to let them have it. Or let them think they have it. Because inevitably they will try to use it. And if you're smart, you can catch them when they do."

Before Andrew could answer, the kitchen timer went off.

"Quarter to nine!" Mrs. Digitalis announced. "You'd better be home to greet your father before my house turns into a pumpkin."

Evie groaned with disappointment. "Can we have another lesson someday?"

"Of course, dear," said Mrs. Digitalis.

With a flurry of good-byes and thank-yous, Andrew and Evie left the house. By now the night had turned cooler, and the smell of a burning fireplace nearby wafted into the yard.

"Next time, let *me* do the talking," Evie said. "I was going to ask her about Mom, but *you* had to open your big mouth."

She stormed away across the lawn toward their house.

But Andrew wasn't listening. He was still thinking about Mrs. Digitalis's words.

Inevitably they will try to use it. And if you're smart, you can catch them when they do.

He knew exactly what he needed to do at school the next day.

Chapter Twelve

Andrew felt his pocket. He wore extra-baggy pants today. He needed the capacity.

If his plan worked, he owed Mrs. Digitalis another packet of seeds.

The morning fog was thick and cool. As Andrew and Jason biked to school, it made eddies of silver vapor around them.

There they were. Baluko and his pals. Waiting at the front door.

"Hey, Jason — you have to sell *all* of that candy for the chess team?" Andrew asked loudly as they locked their bikes to the rack.

Baluko turned toward them. He took a bite out of a half-eaten Three Musketeers bar.

Jason removed a box of assorted chocolates from his backpack. "Well, not all by myself!" he shouted. "I have to distribute candy to the *rest of the team* after school! I have *two other boxes* like this *in my locker*! *Lots* and *lots*

of candy! If we sell them *all*, we'll win a trip to the junior chess championship in Simsbury!"

Jason, Andrew decided, was a terrible actor.

"Ooooh, the juniaw championshipth in Thimthberry!" cooed Baluko. "How thwell!"

As Andrew and Jason rounded the corner of the hallway, Evie and Char were waiting. "Did he hear you?" Evie whispered.

"Yup," Andrew said.

The plan was set. Baluko would not try to steal anything between classes. It would be too crowded. He'd either try to leave in the middle of a class or during lunch, when the hall would be empty.

Between Jason, Evie, Char, and Andrew, they could keep an eye on Baluko all day.

Jason opened his locker and stuffed the candy box onto the shelf. Then he placed his squirt-flower next to it, attached a string from the flower to the inside locker handle, and closed the door. "Perfect. He'll open the door, and the flower will squirt him — with permanent red ink."

"Ink?" Andrew said. "I thought it was just water!"

"We need better evidence than that," Jason suggested.

"But we'll *have* evidence. I'm going to hide in an empty locker, pop out, and photograph him. Remember?"

"What if the camera malfunctions? Or if you have claustrophobia and chicken out?"

"That is absurd. That is absolutely ridiculous." Andrew tried the handle on an abandoned locker opposite Jason's. The door swung open. "Look at this. It's huge. I could live in there. It'll be as comfy as my bedroom. Now, let's take off before Baluko sees us."

They met at the beginning of lunch period. "Well?" Andrew asked.

"He got up to go to the bathroom twice in homeroom and once in Math," Evie said. "I faked a stomachache, volunteered to bring a note to the principal's office, and had a sneezing fit. All three times I was excused to the hallway. I deserved an Oscar. But he didn't go near Jason's locker. The rest of you?"

"He read a comic book in English," Char volunteered.

"He slept through History," Jason said.

Evie nodded. "I think he's going to act at lunch."

"Roger," said Andrew. "I'll be there."

After fifteen minutes in the locker, Andrew was shaking. He wanted to scream. He felt cramped and squashed. He saw green slime monsters in the dark walls and heard the cackling of witches.

And the smell. It hadn't been here at the beginning. What was it? Had something died in here?

Andrew tried to look around, but he could barely move his head. Then he lifted his arms a fraction of an inch.

It was Eau de Andrew. Fifteen minutes of intense, concentrated fear-sweat.

Enough was enough. He had to get out. Now.

He raised the locker handle.

Click.

The thump of footsteps made him freeze. He held the locker door closed.

Baluko. For sure. Andrew could tell by the heavy breathing. And the smell of chocolate.

He peered through the slats. Baluko was looking left and right. Then he sauntered over to Jason's locker and fumbled in his pocket for the universal key.

Hallelujah.

Andrew fingered the telescope, now compressed into its camera shape. He would have to move fast.

A few more seconds, Andrew, he told himself. *You can do it.*

Baluko dropped the key to the floor. He was nervous,

too. Muttering under his breath, he picked it up and inserted it into Jason's lock.

Now.

Andrew pushed the door open and leaped out.

His left foot caught the edge of the locker. The floor rushed toward him. With a yell, he threw out his arms to stop the fall.

The telescope-camera went flying.

"What the — ?" Baluko said.

Andrew hit the floor on his stomach as the telescope clattered to the tiles. He lunged forward, reaching out.

But Baluko leaned down and scooped it off the floor.

"Aha!" Andrew cried out, scrambling to his feet. "I caught you red-handed!"

"You did?" Baluko said innocently. "What did you catch me doing?"

Andrew glanced at Jason's locker. It was still shut.

Baluko shoved the key in his pocket. "Looks like maybe I caught *you*, Wall. Planning to cut class by hiding in a locker."

"*What*? I never cut class!"

"Then why would you be in a locker? Not that I want to know, but I'm sure that's what the principal will ask when I tell him I found you hiding from your teacher while I went to the bathroom."

"You wouldn't. That's a lie!"

Baluko examined the camera. He extended the telescope lens and looked through. "This is cool. Well, let's see. I just *might* agree to keep my mouth shut . . . for a price. Like, maybe, I don't know, this little gadget?"

"I can't give you my key *and* my telescope!" Andrew squeaked.

"Hey, I could have asked for your bike," Baluko replied.

"But, but I . . ."

"I tell you what, smart guy," Baluko said. "You disappear on the count of three, leaving me this Cracker Jack toy, and I will consider not reporting you. One . . ."

"You can't do this!" Andrew protested.

"Two . . ."

Andrew turned and began walking.

This was a total disgrace. Some spy. They would all be mad at him now. Jason, Evie, Char, Mrs. Digitalis, Pop — and the principal, if Baluko reneged on his pledge.

Which wouldn't surprise Andrew.

Behind him he could hear keys clinking; Baluko was reaching into his pocket.

"Three."

Click.

The lock. Jason's lock.

Andrew rounded the corner and waited . . .

"AUUGHHHHH!" came Baluko's voice.

Andrew peeked back. At the end of the hall, Baluko stood in front of the open locker, frantically trying to wipe the red ink off his shirt. "This is brand-new! My mom's going to kill me!"

The telescope-camera was on the floor. Baluko had dropped it. Andrew ran toward it. Before Baluko could look, Andrew picked it up off the floor. "Say cheese!" he said.

Andrew pointed and clicked.

"It's a *camera*?" Baluko asked.

"This'll be a great picture," Andrew said, backing away. "You standing in front of Jason's locker, wide open, with a key in the lock. Attempted robbery. Hm. Juvenile court or just a suspension?"

"Come on, all he has in that locker is *candy*. You wouldn't rat on me, Wall."

The end-of-the-period bell resounded. Down the hallway, the cafeteria doors swung open.

Andrew pretended to think. "Maybe I wouldn't. But there's a price." He held out his hand.

Baluko reached into his pocket. As the first wave of kids came clambering out, he put the key into Andrew's palm.

Chapter Thirteen

"I slaughtered him — *akakakakak* — vanquished him until he was a quivering mass of helpless protoplasm, begging at my feet!" Andrew cried, riding his bike through the soupy fog.

"Don't forget," Jason shouted, pedaling hard to catch up, "if it weren't for that ink, he wouldn't have been caught!"

"Andrew, slow down!" Evie called out.

He is soaring, thirty thousand feet above the ground, returning from the deadliest mission of all. Soon his flight path veers south, and he has to tip his wings farewell to Colonel Jason, who veers away.

As Andrew and Evie rolled up their driveway, Evie stopped short.

Mrs. Digitalis was at the edge of her garden, silently watching them. Without a word, she turned and walked inside, dropping a squarish white piece of paper among the tomato plants.

"Oops, she might need that." Andrew ran across the lawn and fished around in the plants for the paper.

It was an envelope, with a message scribbled on the front:

A & E — OPEN IN PRIVATE.

He sped back and showed it to Evie. "Come on."

In the living room, Andrew ripped open the envelope and pulled out a tasteful card decorated with a watercolor still life of a flower bouquet. Tucked inside was a message:

> Lesson Number 2:
> A. Look closely at everything.
> B. Never assume you know who has sent an unidentified package until you have examined every item.
> C. If you see your mother before I do, tell her that the foxglove didn't take, but it is a resilient flower and will rise again.
> D. Best of luck.
> — A. D.

Folded up in the envelope, along with the message, was a page ripped from a book about plants — a photo and description of foxglove.

"What does it mean?" Andrew asked.

"I don't know," Evie said. "Sounds like she's saying good-bye to us."

"Can't be. Maybe it's a code."

"Not everything is a code, Andrew. Maybe it's a lesson. We should follow it."

"Okay. The first part, Part A: 'Look closely at everything.' I'll look closely at this, you look at the clipping." Andrew held up the note to the light.

Evie smoothed out the clipping. "Foxglove?"

She turned it around to show Andrew:

Foxglove
A perennial, or self-seeding, herb characterized by hanging tubular flowers, often of a violet hue. A member of the figwort family, the foxglove is known by the genus name *Digitalis*.

"Funny," Andrew said. "No wonder she made a face when we showed her the packet. She's famous. Her name is in print."

"Digitalis . . . foxglove . . ." Evie murmured. "Don't

you think it's strange, Andrew? We arrive here, in this house next to a woman who knows Mom, whose name matches the name of flowers we get anonymously in the mail, in a package which happens to contain a bunch of spy material?"

"Maybe Uncle Frank *is* a spy. Maybe Mom's staying with him — and they're trying to send Mrs. Digitalis a message through us."

"Maybe." Evie turned to Mrs. Digitalis's note again and read aloud: "'B. Never assume you know who has sent an unidentified package until you have examined every item.'"

They both raced upstairs. As Andrew disappeared into his bedroom, Evie took a detour. On a hunch, she knelt by her bed and reached under her mattress.

Looking over her shoulder, Evie felt her hidden desk key. Then she pulled out a tattered sheet of legal paper. She unfolded it carefully. And for about the thousandth time in ten months, she read the note her mom had left in the kitchen the day she disappeared.

This time, she saw something new.

Evie sped back into Andrew's room. He was sitting on his bed, the contents of the box laid out before him. "Andrew, I have something! Can you read me the last paragraph of Uncle Frank's note?"

"Sure." Andrew bent over the paper. " 'It's too soon to know if I affected the children,' " he read. " 'Love, as you know — more than stories about birds and plants, myths and movies — works miracles. A picture forms, but confused, because you are missing.' "

She held out the letter. "Now read this — the P.S. that Mom left."

"You have that?"

"Don't worry, I kept it safe."

Andrew took it gently and skimmed to the end.

P.S. You will hear from me soon. And when you do, remember:

11 11 11 :
A picture forms
Without you —
And it's all a jumble.

"The wording is so alike," Andrew remarked.

"That's my point," Evie said. "What if Uncle Frank *didn't* send us this note?"

Andrew set the note down. "But the return address . . ."

"Alaska, with a letter F . . . We assumed it was from him. But there was no postmark, Andrew."

"So you think . . . ?" Andrew's heart was banging.

"All those references in the note," Evie barreled on. "*On the Waterfront,* William Tell, Father Christmas. Yeah, it sounds like Uncle Frank. Sort of. But when you think about it . . ."

"It's *so* Mom," Andrew said softly.

"Not to mention the story — a woman trying to say something to two kids who can't hear her. Saying she must leave for awhile. Telling the kids to stick together. That's a message to us. Andrew, I can't be sure, but . . ."

"Do you know what this *means*, Evie?"

Evie's eyes were moist. "She's alive."

"And she's . . ." Andrew had to breathe steadily, to allow himself the words he never expected to say. "She's trying to reach us."

"It fits, Andrew, it all fits. Where she writes 'this violet bird,' that's got to be Mrs. Digitalis, dressed in purple . . . 'The plant and bird are identical.' . . . The plant is foxglove — Digitalis."

"Mom knew we'd meet her."

"But how?"

Andrew looked at the two pieces of paper, the story and their mother's note from a year ago. "These two phrases, from Mom's old note and this one — 'A picture forms without you — and it's all a jumble' and 'a picture forms, but confused, because you are missing.' Why are they so alike? Is this some kind of code?"

"Remember what Mrs. Digitalis said: Certain words are really instructions," Evie reminded him. "They help you unlock the key to a coded message."

" 'Backward,' meaning to spell a word backward, or 'mix-up,' meaning to rearrange letters," said Andrew.

"One message says 'jumble,' the other says 'confused'!"

Andrew scratched his head. "So something in each message needs to be rearranged?"

"Exactly!" Evie replied. "And each one contains an identical phrase, word for word."

" 'A picture forms'?"

"What do we get if we jumble those letters?"

Andrew ran to his computer. "Give me a nanosecond or two."

"What are you doing?"

"Running the anagram program. Pop downloaded it. You punch in words and it scrambles them into other words." Andrew quickly tapped out the three words A PICTURE FORMS on his keyboard. A moment later the results flashed on the screen. " 'Campfire tours,' " he read, " 'rump factories,' 'a piecrust form,' 'a cure from spit,' nah, nothing makes sense."

"Maybe we picked the wrong phrase," Evie asked.

They both stared at the two sheets again. "Let's break this down," Andrew said. "Each sentence has three parts. The parts about the jumble and confused, that's an instruction to unscramble the other part, 'a picture forms.' So far, so good. But there's another part to both messages."

With a pencil, Evie marked them up:

A picture forms

Without you —

And it's all a jumble.

A picture forms, but confused, because you are missing.

" 'Without you' and 'because you are missing,' " Evie said. "Similar, I guess. They both have the word 'you.' But what do they mean?"

Andrew thought a moment. "They could be instructions. Maybe we're supposed to do something to the word 'you.' "

" 'Without' and 'missing,' sounds like we're supposed to take away the word 'you' from something." Evie stared closely at both messages. "From 'a picture forms'?"

"You can't subtract the letters Y-O-U from 'a picture forms,' " Andrew muttered.

Evie grinned. "But the word 'you' sounds like —"

"The *letter* U!" Andrew exclaimed. He moved the cursor to the middle of the phrase and pressed DELETE, removing the U from "picture."

The monitor read A PICTRE FORMS.

"Now what?" Evie said.

"Let's run the anagram program again," Andrew suggested.

In seconds the program spat back a list of choices. Evie looked over Andrew's shoulder as he read: " 'Armpit forces,' 'I'm for carpets,' 'spice from rat,' 'strip of cream,' 'prime factors.' "

"Wait," Evie said. "Maybe that's it, Andrew."

"Prime factors?"

"Yes! Prime numbers you multiply together! Mrs. Digitalis's code keys were all math, right? So maybe this one is, too."

Andrew's face turned gray. "I hate higher math. What's a prime number?"

"It can only be divided by itself and one, like three,

five, seven, eleven," Evie explained. "Now, take a number like twenty-one. It's not a prime number. But it has prime factors."

"Seven times three?" Andrew said.

"You're a genius."

"So we're supposed to find prime factors? Of *what*, Evie? We don't have a number."

Thump.

From outside came the sound of a thick door slamming shut.

Andrew opened his window and looked out. Mrs. Digitalis was walking quickly from the garage to her car. She wore sunglasses and a tight black turtleneck with dark pants.

"She's in a hurry," Andrew remarked.

Evie was staring across the driveway. "Andrew, look."

Andrew glanced in the direction of her gaze, at Mrs. Digitalis's office.

It was empty. The computer, the papers — all gone.

Chapter Fourteen

She couldn't leave them.

Not now.

Evie watched Mrs. Digitalis hurrying across the lawn. Fumbling for keys.

She was in a hurry. Her house was empty. In a minute she would disappear from their lives without a trace.

No. With *one* trace.

A note from Mom.

Like the other note. From another house. Another time, impossibly distant. A ripped yellow sheet, bright and new, in her brother's trembling hand.

A note. And then nothing.

The nothing was the worst part.

And it was about to happen again.

Mom was close this time, closer than she'd been in a year. So close Evie could feel her smile. Mrs. Digitalis was the connection. The key. She couldn't abandon them now.

"Come on, Andrew." Evie ran out the bedroom door.

She took the stairs two at a time and barged out the front door.

Mrs. Digitalis was in her car. It coughed to life.

"Wait!" Evie grabbed the handle on the passenger door.

The window rolled down. "I left you a note!" Mrs. Digitalis shouted.

"Where are you going?" Evie demanded.

"I don't have time!" Mrs. Digitalis replied.

"Why?" Evie said. *"Are you going to our mom?"*

Mrs. Digitalis gunned the accelerator. "I will write to you when I can. But I must go. Now."

Andrew backed away. "Evie, she's serious."

"So am I." Evie yanked open the passenger door. She grabbed Andrew by the arm, shoved him in the backseat, and jumped in after.

"What are you — *get out of my car!*" Mrs. Digitalis stammered.

Evie looked her in the eye. "Tell us where you're going, or we're not moving."

"*We?*" Andrew said.

"There's no time!" Mrs. Digitalis hissed.

Evie folded her arms and sat back in the seat.

Mrs. Digitalis's eyes darted upward, through the rear window. For a moment. Then she spun around and shifted to Drive. "All right, then, fasten your belts."

SCREEEEE . . .

The car lurched out of the driveway. Andrew fell against Evie, pinning her against the right rear side.

"*Get . . . off . . .*" Evie shoved him back and sat up. Outside the window, a stop sign flew by. A car honked long and loud.

Each maple tree on Lakeview Avenue whooshed by as they passed.

Click. Andrew put his seat belt on. His hands shook.

Mrs. Digitalis's eyes darted toward the rearview mirror. She was approaching a red light at the corner of Huron Avenue. A truck trundled toward the intersection from the left. "Hold on, kids."

She pulled the steering wheel to the right. Evie vaulted out of her seat, hitting her head against the ceiling. She saw the grille of the truck outside Andrew's window, heard the shriek of tires and the blast of an industrial-size horn.

"*Evie, put your seat belt on!*" Andrew cried out.

Evie scrambled into her seat and pulled the belt around her. Huron was a four-lane street, two in either direction. Mrs. Digitalis was picking up speed. Her eyes were locked on the mirror.

Not on Evie. On something else.

Evie turned. A navy blue car with dark-tinted windows was directly behind them, matching their speed.

"You're being *followed*?" Evie said.

"Looks like it," Mrs. Digitalis replied.

Andrew nudged his sister in the ribs, pointing out the window. "Look!"

Their father's car was passing in the far lane, going the other direction. Heading home.

"*Pop!*" Evie yelled.

"Ssssh!" said Andrew. "If he sees us, we are in big trouble!"

"You don't know how true that is," Mrs. Digitalis said.

Evie leaned forward. "We know Mom is alive, Mrs. Digitalis. She sent us that package. With the telescope."

"And the note," Andrew added. "She mentioned you, too. Who are you?"

EEEEEE . . .

Mrs. Digitalis swerved around a line of cars, then turned right onto Melwyn Road.

Melwyn led out of town. A cluster of gas stations gave way to tightly packed houses and small farms along a winding road. "You are correct," Mrs. Digitalis said. "She is alive. And in hiding."

Evie gripped her brother's hand. "Hiding from what?"

"Not what," Mrs. Digitalis replied. "Whom. Your mother was a great asset to The Company. Too great, as it turned out. She could find information about anything, no matter how well concealed. She happened to find out some things about The Company itself. Things she wasn't supposed to know. She had to get away before they found out. She did . . . and they did."

"Do you know where she is?" Andrew pressed. "Can you take us to see her?"

Mrs. Digitalis shook her head. "I have no idea where to find her. I've been trying for a year. When you told me who you were, I praised my lucky stars. I figured she would try to contact you, but I knew she couldn't do it overtly. That's why I started to train you to look for clues. Codes."

"The seeds," Andrew said. "She knew you'd recognize them. You'd know where they came from."

"What about the telescope?" Evie said.

"Your mother was wily. Perhaps she knew you would use it to notice things, photograph them." Mrs. Digitalis cracked a wry smile. "Maybe she thought you'd keep an eye on me. Hang on."

The road forked ahead, forming a triangle. The right side was a dirt path, the left was paved. The top of the triangle was a paved road that cut from one road to the other. Mrs. Digitalis stepped on the gas and turned right, onto the dirt path, then slammed on the brakes.

The car swerved from side to side, sending up a cloud of dust. Without stopping, Mrs. Digitalis gunned the accelerator and turned left, across the top of the triangle.

In a moment they were on the paved road, heading toward the next town. To their right dust billowed upward, shrinking farther into the distance.

"That ought to fool them," Mrs. Digitalis said. "They'll think we continued down the dirt road."

"Who's they?" Evie asked.

"Are they the same people Mom's hiding from?" Andrew pressed.

"I can't give you the answers you need," Mrs. Digitalis replied. "You will have to keep your ears open. If your mother has gotten through to you, she will try again. They will be onto her, though. You can bet on that."

"What if they find out?" Evie asked. "What will they do to her?"

"She will take precautions," Mrs. Digitalis said. "The problem is, will you? You must recognize when she is sending you a message. It won't be obvious. If I could stay with you, I'd train you properly. But I can't. At the next town I will leave you at the bus station, and you'll go home on your own. When you get there, you must dedicate yourself. You must keep her secrets and tell no one."

"But Pop needs to know," Andrew said. "And he'll help us —"

"*Under no circumstances,*" Mrs. Digitalis said sharply. "Involving him will jeopardize your mother's safety. Perhaps her life. Remember, you are your mother's only hope. She cannot get back without your help."

The words seemed to close around Evie like a fist. "But we're kids. How can we do this without you?"

"I gave you the tools you'll need for now. More will come your way soon enough." A ring of sweat had formed across Mrs. Digitalis's forehead. Her eyes darted toward the rearview mirror.

Evie and Andrew turned. They were cresting a hill now. Far behind them, coming over the top of the previous hill, were two cars.

Mrs. Digitalis pressed the accelerator to the floor on the downhill. They were approaching the town of Melwyn. An antiques store whizzed on the right, a tract development on the left. In the distance, a train whistle. Closer, a warning bell.

DING-DING-DING-DING . . .

Andrew and Evie faced forward. Mrs. Digitalis murmured something under her breath. A hundred yards ahead of them, just past a white-shingled grocery store, railroad-crossing gates began to descend across the road.

The train was approaching from the right, slowly. The locomotive was silver and sleek, its headlights dappled by the passing trees. Behind it, a line of boxcars snaked out of sight.

Evie felt the car speed up.

"Mrs. Digitalis?" she said, her voice catching.

"What are you doing?" Andrew yelled.

The gates were down.

Another car pulled to a stop, ahead of them. A guard raced out of the shingled house, waving frantically.

"Hold tight," said Mrs. Digitalis.

She yanked the steering wheel to the left. The car hopped the curb into an abandoned, weed-strewn parking lot.

The train track, unblocked by a gate, was just ahead of them.

Evie closed her eyes. And she shrieked.

Chapter Fifteen

Evie heard the clang of the bell. The locomotive horn blasted so loudly, it seemed inside her brain.

The car had stopped.

"Evie?" Andrew said. "Are you okay?"

Evie opened her eyes. Her brother was doubled over, his head between his knees.

She sat up.

Mrs. Digitalis was gone. The driver's side door was open.

In a spray of gravel, two cars pulled into the parking lot beside them. Out of the first one jumped the dark-haired woman and the balding man who had been inside Mrs. Digitalis's house. They sprinted toward the passing train, which was picking up speed.

Just then Evie noticed the figure running alongside the train itself, with the loping strides of a long-distance runner.

"Mrs. Digitalis?" Andrew said.

A shock of white hair billowed out from behind her. She reached out for a handhold on the side of an open freight car, but the train was going too fast.

As the next handhold passed her, Mrs. Digitalis lunged.

Her fingers closed around the metal bar. She grabbed with her other hand. Her legs lifted off the ground.

As the train passed a hulking brick warehouse, Evie saw Mrs. Digitalis's feet vanish inside the train car.

The woman and the man, who had been joined by two others, were running back to their cars now. Evie pushed Andrew's head down and ducked.

But the four pursuers had no interest in Evie and Andrew. They jumped into their cars and took off across the lot, following the train.

Evie sat, not moving. The day's events began replaying in her head. By the railroad gate, a small crowd of people stared in their direction, mumbling among themselves.

"What are they staring at?" Andrew said. "Haven't they ever seen two kids in a Volkswagen bug abandoned by an old woman who outruns a train?"

Evie unbuckled her seat belt. "Come on, Andrew. Pop's probably thinking we're dead or something. We'd better start walking home."

"Walking?" Andrew exclaimed. "We won't get there until the weekend!"

Evie pushed the passenger seat forward. As she leaned over it to open the door, a car roared up from behind them.

"Evie?" a voice shouted from an open window.

She climbed out and turned.

Pop was already out of his car, running toward her.

She put out her arms and let him lift her off the ground.

"Oh, sweetie, are you all right?" he asked.

Evie just nodded, burying her face in his shoulder, feeling the warmth of her own tears seep into the fabric of his jacket.

"I'm okay, too, Pop," Andrew said, climbing out of the car.

Pop knelt, gathering both of them in a tight embrace. "I am so relieved."

"You're not mad?" Evie said.

"Mad?" Her father shook his head, his eyes moistening. "A year ago, when your mother disappeared, I worried that whoever took her — if someone did — would come after you. For a year, I've hated to leave you alone."

"That's why you didn't want us talking to strangers," Evie said. "And we did."

"How did you find us?" Andrew asked.

Pop looked off into the distance. "I never trusted that woman. Digitalis. When I saw her doing sixty on Huron Avenue, with you two in the backseat, I nearly had a heart attack. I pulled a U-turn, but she was long gone. Fortunately those other two cars were after her, too, and I managed to follow them."

The other cars.

Evie looked over her shoulder. They'd chase after Mrs. Digitalis for awhile. Maybe they'd find her. Maybe not.

If they didn't, they'd be back.

For her and Andrew.

"Pop, let's go home," she said. "Now."

"Sure," her father said, standing up. "Home sweet home."

It was dark by the time they got home, stopping for a pizza on the way. Dinner was quiet. Normal.

Mr. Wall must have toasted their health with soda a dozen times.

When he went up to his room afterward to make some phone calls, Evie and Andrew sat out in the back-yard.

Mrs. Digitalis's house peaked over the tops of the hedges, looking barren and sad.

"Evie?" Andrew said. "Where did it all go — her stuff?"

Evie shrugged. "It must be somewhere close by. I didn't hear moving vans."

Andrew walked to the hedge and peeked through. In Mrs. Digitalis's backyard, a shed stood black against the moonlit night.

"Can we do it?" Evie whispered.

Andrew looked toward their house. "You get a couple of flashlights. I'll meet you at the garage."

He squeezed through the hedge into Mrs. Digitalis's yard. He hadn't seen the shed up close, but even in the darkness he could tell it wasn't what it appeared to be. What seemed like weathered wood from a distance was actually some kind of molding. The door hinges were the size of Pringles canisters, the latch a bolt of thick metal.

As Evie returned with two lit flashlights, Andrew rapped his knuckle against the wall. "Steel."

Evie tried the latch. "Locked, too."

Crouching, Andrew examined the latch. Beneath it was a metal hood, just large enough to fit a hand under. Inside the hood was a reinforced keyhole.

Andrew reached into his pocket and took out the master key he had taken back from Baluko earlier that day.

He knelt by the door. Evie shone her flashlight into

the metal hood, illuminating the keyhole. Andrew stuck his hand underneath and inserted the key. "It's the wrong size," he said, flicking the edge of the key head. "This is probably some industrial-grade, military —"

Click.

With a deep groan, the door swung open.

Evie and Andrew backed away.

"Hello?" Evie called out.

An angry twittering answered from above.

"Bats," Andrew said. "Yuck."

Evie stepped inside. "We may have to wash our hair tonight."

Andrew followed close behind. They swung their lights around. Over an old workbench, a set of shelves held different size nails and bolts. Rusty tools hung on a rack.

At the end of the workbench, a purple blanket covered a bulky object. Evie reached out and pulled it off.

Mrs. Digitalis's computer was underneath. "Can we plug it in?" she said.

But Andrew didn't answer. From under the blanket, a squarish paper object had fallen to the floor. Shining his light on it, he picked it up and looked at the flower printed on it.

"Foxglove," he said, reading the label. "This is the seed packet we gave Mrs. Digitalis."

He shone the flashlight into the packet. No seeds remained, but on the inside, a note had been written in bold marker:

111111
Foxglove,
Teach them.
X

"Eleven, eleven, eleven," Andrew murmured.

"This is definitely from Mom!" Evie blurted out. "November eleventh, eleven years old! She wrote that in her note to us, too!"

The sight of his mother's handwriting made Andrew dizzy. He propped himself up against the workbench, the events of the last few days bombarding his brain. The chase, the codes, the stolen bike, the cramped locker, Baluko and Jason, and the key — and now two communications from Mom in one night. Two very strange communications.

He stared at the note, reading every letter and number, imagining his mother's hand putting pen to paper, trying to feel her near.

But it was hard. These notes were so unlike her. Mom

was a *clear* person. She said what she meant. These notes made no sense. *Absolutely no sense.*

X? Why X?

And why did she write that number — 11 11 11? That was a private number between Mom, Evie, and Andrew. It wasn't Mrs. Digitalis's business.

"'Teach them'?" Evie said. "Teach them what? Codes?"

Andrew nodded. "She and Mrs. Digitalis worked on codes."

Andrew swallowed his words. He stared at the number.

Why hadn't he seen it before?

"Evie?" he said. "On Mom's note? The one she left us a year ago? Where did she write eleven-eleven-eleven?"

"At the end," Evie replied.

"I mean, *where* at the end?"

"Before the stuff about 'a picture forms,' the stuff we thought was a code."

Andrew's hands were trembling. "It *is* a code."

"What?"

"Evie, what are the prime factors of eleven-eleven-eleven — one hundred eleven thousand one hundred eleven?"

*   *   *

They were in Andrew's bedroom in no time.

Pop wasn't in his room. He must have gone back to work. It was Evie who came up with the solution first:

$$111,111 = 3 \times 7 \times 11 \times 13 \times 37$$

"Okay, now what?" Evie asked.

"Well, think about the fraction code," Andrew said. "If we had one-sixth, we read every sixth word."

"This isn't a fraction," Evie reminded him. "These are factors. There are five of them."

Andrew stared at the coded message, then at the numbers: 3, 7, 11, 13, 37. "Well, 'three' could mean every third word, and 'seven' every seventh."

"Ugh. That's complicated."

"Let's number the words, the way Mrs. Digitalis did," Andrew suggested. "It'll come to us."

He took out his pencil and carefully began to write numbers under the words in each line:

```
Alas!  My  dear,  distant,  dis-
  1     2    3                  4         5
tracted little ones don't hear as I
   5       6      7      8      9   10  11
speak. Am I not loud enough? No, I
  12    13 14 15  16     17      18 , 19
realize to my chagrin that they're
   20   21 22    23     24     25
too far. In another world. I sigh,
 26  27  28  29      30     31  32
and then all of a sudden, I spy
 33   34  35  36 37
```

"Every third word is 'Dear . . . little . . . hear . . . speak . . .'" Evie said. "Makes no sense."

"What if we just take the third word, seventh word, eleventh word, thirteenth word, and thirty-seventh word?" Andrew said.

He counted, then drew a line under each:

```
     Alas!  My  dear,  distant,  dis-
           1    2     3                 4           5
     tracted little ones don't hear as I
        5       6      7      8     9   10 11
     speak. Am I not loud enough? No, I
       12    13 14 15  16     17      18 , 19
     realize to my chagrin that they're
       20    21 22   23     24    25
     too far. In another world. I sigh,
      26  27  28   29      30     31 32
     and then all of a sudden, I spy
      33   34   35  36 37
```

"'Dear ones,'" Evie read. "'I am a . . .' I am a *what*?"

"I don't know!" Andrew said. "What do we do from here?"

"Keep numbering!" Evie suggested.

"But we already got to thirty-seven!"

"Start over from one! Do the whole thing that way!"

Evie watched over Andrew's shoulder as he completed the entire letter.

```
     Alas!  My  dear,  distant,  dis-
           1    2     3                 4           5
     tracted little ones don't hear as I
        5       6      7      8     9   10 11
```

speak. Am I not loud enough? No, I realize to my chagrin that they're too far. In another world. I sigh, and then all of a sudden, I spy something that I cannot adequately describe. "I'll tell, to you only, of this violet bird's splendors," I say to the two children. "It has intelligence and will sing for you—so go to where it is, I beseech you! I am afraid, though, you'll need all your energy and charm to make it understand who you are." I look to see if they understand me; I'm not certain.

I can't help but notice foxglove afoot. "This gift will be available to assist if you know how to find it," I say. "The plant and bird, you see, are identical. Whatever grows the closest to one's home may be useful. Be careful, though. Like William Tell, who certainly had no intent, one presumes, to cause harm,

the people nearest to you may prove
ultimately to be your undoing."

    With these words I leave, frus-
trated but not without hope—even
with my doubts. Father Christmas I
don't expect for another few
months, but the weather has turned
cold and I must leave for a while.
Like that fabled jolly old saint, I
will parcel things out. Don't rush
and don't worry—these words may,
we'll agree, be the wisest that
can be said—along with Marlon
Brando's advice from ON THE WATER-
FRONT: Keep fighting. Always be a
contender. Gain strength together.

    It's too soon to know if I af-
fected the children. Love, as you
know—more than stories about birds
and plants, myths and movies—works
miracles. A picture forms, but confused, because you are missing.

    I spy, you spy. X marks the spot.

They stared at the results. Andrew swallowed a frog in his throat. He read slowly, putting in punctuation where it belonged: " 'Dear ones: I am a spy. Cannot tell you where I am. Need your help. Foxglove will assist you.' "

"Foxglove — Digitalis," Evie said.

" 'Be careful. Tell no one,' " Andrew went on, " 'not even Father. Expect another parcel. Don't worry, we'll be together soon. I love you. Spy X.' "

"Spy X? Is that what we're supposed to call her?"

"Who cares? The important thing is, she's alive. She knows where we are."

Evie's lip began to quiver, but her eyes said Fourth of July. Mom was trying to reach them. They were close — so close. "I know, I know! But what do we do now? What about Mrs. Digitalis? What about us? Those people who chased her — do they want us, too?"

Downstairs, the front door slammed.

Evie and Andrew clutched each other's hands.

They heard footsteps clomp across the living room. The opening of a window. Silence.

Bedsheets. That's how you escaped. If they came upstairs, Andrew thought, he and Evie could tie bedsheets together and bail out his window. But would they reach the ground?

Thump. Thump. Thump. Thump.

"Evie? Andrew?"

Pop's voice. It was *Pop*.

Andrew nearly collapsed with relief. "We're up here!" he called.

"Get your things together," Pop said, "at once."

"Where are we going?" Evie called.

She and Andrew went to the top of the stairs. Their father looked haggard. His shirttails hung out and his tie was askew. "We're moving."

"Now?" Andrew asked.

"Something's come up." Pop wiped his neck with a handkerchief. "Sorry. Be down here with all your stuff in twenty minutes."

"Twenty minutes?" Andrew said.

"What about school?" Evie pleaded.

"My bike!" Andrew added.

"We'll send for everything later." He looked at his watch. "Nineteen minutes."

Andrew and Evie looked out into the foggy night. A car glided by, and Andrew felt his heart jump, but it sped off into the night.

Evie ran into her room, leaving him alone.

He took a deep breath. He reached under his bed, took out the box from Mom, and put it in his suitcase.

About the Author

Peter Lerangis is the author of *Smiler's Bones*, a historical novel; *Watchers*, an award-winning science-fiction/mystery series; *Antarctica*, a two-book exploration adventure; and *Abracadabra*, a hilarious series for younger readers. He has written several adaptations of hit movies, including *The Sixth Sense*. He is a Harvard graduate and lives in New York City with his wife, Tina deVaron, and their two sons, Nick and Joe.